The Sweet
Remnants of Summer

The Sweet
Remnants of Summer

ALEXANDER
McCALL SMITH

Little, Brown

LITTLE, BROWN

First published in Great Britain in 2022 by Little, Brown

1 3 5 7 9 10 8 6 4 2

A CIP catalogue record for this book
is available from the British Library.

HB ISBN 978-1-408-71717-2
C format 978-1-408-71718-9

Typeset in Bembo by MRules
Printed and bound in Great Britain by
Clays Ltd, Elcograf S.p.A

Papers used by Little, Brown are from well-managed forests
and other responsible sources.

Little, Brown
An imprint of
Little, Brown Book Group
Carmelite House
50 Victoria Embankment
London EC4Y 0DZ

An Hachette UK Company
www.hachette.co.uk

www.littlebrown.co.uk

This book is for Sarah and Gordon Brown.

1

'Is it possible, do you think, to be too good?'

Isabel Dalhousie asked her husband Jamie this question while he was standing in the shower, washing his hair. It was typical of the unexpected questions that Isabel sometimes posed, without warning, and on any subject that happened to come to mind. 'Was Wittgenstein really as brilliant as people thought him to be?' she had asked a few days earlier. 'Or were people simply wrong-footed by his insistence that all the questions that had preoccupied them were, in fact, meaningless?' This question, addressed to nobody in particular, being more of an utterance, a soliloquy perhaps, than an actual question, was intercepted by her housekeeper, Grace, who had thought for no more than a few moments before replying, 'Who knows? But don't forget to buy butter, please – we've almost run out.'

When this question about good was asked, Jamie was using a new shampoo Isabel had purchased on impulse, swayed by the sheer effrontery of its packaging. *Hair care for the thinking man,* the label announced, before claiming, *The shampoo Einstein would have used*. That made her laugh out loud, causing the assistant behind the counter, and a woman browsing the vitamin shelves, to look up with surprise. Isabel had become aware of their glances, and had felt obliged to explain. Those who erupt in sudden, private laughter often feel they must say why.

'It's just that one is not always struck by what one reads on shampoo bottles,' she said, flourishing the bottle. And then added, 'In fact, shampoo bottles make rather dull reading . . . usually.'

The woman behind her had a sense of humour. 'This one,' she said, 'is obviously a rather better read.'

Isabel laughed again, although this brief exchange was lost on the young assistant, who was busying herself with keying the details of a refund into the card reader. That was the problem with being nineteen, thought Isabel: nineteen-year-olds take themselves – and the world – far too seriously, and have yet to discover how unintentionally funny both can be.

She had shown the bottle to the woman behind her and they had both shaken their heads over the hyperbolic language of the label. The manufacturers' pitch was clear enough: this was a shampoo aimed at men rather than women, and was intended to imply that if you were intelligent – as most people like to think they are – then this was the shampoo for you. There might also have been an additional, subliminal promise: that the use of this particular shampoo was of some benefit to the brain; a message that could not be spelled out, of course, given truth in advertising considerations, but it could be implied. And so, in the same way as eating fish is said to improve brain function, using the right shampoo might have the effect of improving mental acuity. Perhaps this entirely meretricious marketing strategy actually had women in mind – on the assumption that even a shampoo aimed at men would in most cases be bought by women, for their men. And there must be many women, perhaps the majority, who secretly – or not so secretly in some cases – wished that the man in their lives might be just a little bit brighter. 'Not that I wish I'd married Einstein,' such a woman might say, 'but sometimes . . .' And there would then follow a brief, wistful sigh; not enough to express real dissatisfaction, but sufficiently pointed to remind us that inequality of intelligence can be one of the rocks just below the surface of an otherwise untroubled relationship.

She had bought the shampoo and had meant to point out to Jamie its peculiar claims. He, though, had used it without comment, probably without reading the label. He was unfussy about these things: soap was soap, toothpaste was toothpaste, and shampoo, for all its braggadocio, was simply something you put on your hair, left there for a moment or two, and then rinsed off.

Now he was doing just that, standing under the shower in the bathroom just off the main bedroom in their Edinburgh house, while a speaker he had placed on the bathroom cabinet played the spring movement from Vivaldi's *Four Seasons*. She watched him fondly. He had few faults, but one of them, perhaps, was a propensity to spend far too long in the shower. This had prompted, on one occasion, a warning from Isabel that he could wash away all the natural oils that stand between the skin and its enemies – harsh sunlight, unfriendly microbes, and the gradual wear and tear of the elements.

'Are you suggesting I might *dissolve*?' replied Jamie.

'You know what I mean,' Isabel retorted.

'It would be rather a pleasant way of leaving this world,' Jamie said. 'To dissolve. It has a slightly Buddhist ring to it. You'd dissolve into the air about you. Your molecules would

3

float off like . . . like Chinese lanterns. That, I think, is how Buddhists think about the way we end our lives. We dissolve.'

Isabel pictured one of those small paper lanterns, its little fire heating the trapped air, rising gracefully against a night sky. That would be the soul – feather light at last, freed of its worldly burdens.

'Dissolve?' she mused. 'Yes, possibly. But people think, rather, of ascending – if they're lucky . . .'

'Or descending, if they're not quite so lucky.'

'Precisely.' She reminded herself, though, that the Greeks believed that everybody descended into the underworld, even if bound for the Elysian Fields. And then they must pay the ferryman: would plastic be acceptable to Charon?

But now it was not issues of eschatology that concerned her, but a question of morality. She was, after all, a philosopher, the editor of the *Review of Applied Ethics*, and Jamie was used to her asking questions of this sort at odd and unexpected times.

Now he repeated her question. 'Is it possible to be too good?'

'Yes,' said Isabel.

'Why do you ask?' Jamie enquired from beneath the shower rose.

'I've been wondering why we dislike people who are just *too good*.'

'Do we?'

She was sure we did. 'People like that make us feel uncomfortable.'

She paused. Jamie had turned off the shower and was reaching out for his towel. She passed it to him. Not an ounce of spare flesh, she thought. My Apollo. And, like Apollo, for a moment he seemed to glow in her eyes.

'Do you mean people who are a bit pi?' said Jamie, using the abbreviation of *pious* that Isabel found so expressive. *Pi* was a wonderful, almost onomatopoeic word, reflecting the sound that she imagined might be made by the pursing of the lips in moral self-satisfaction.

Isabel nodded. 'Yes, people who are annoyingly good. They can be so smug.'

Jamie towelled himself roughly. 'That could be Annie in the orchestra,' he said. 'She adopts a pained expression when anybody mentions having a good time. She plays the oboe. She's pretty good – musically, that is – but, oh, her holier than thou attitude gets on our nerves. It really does.'

Isabel said that she, too, had known somebody like that in her student days. 'He was such a pain,' she said. 'Always disapproving of others – telling them what to do. And then he was caught driving while intoxicated and had to appear in court. We all went to his trial – everybody who knew him – and we sat in the public benches and grinned. Somebody sent out an invitation, properly printed, reading, *You are cordially invited to the trial of Roger Mason on a charge of drunken driving. Suit or cocktail dress.*'

'Pure Schadenfreude,' said Jamie. 'But he'd asked for it, I suppose.'

'He was so ashamed,' Isabel said. 'We should have felt guilty, enjoying his discomfort like that, but we didn't. I regret it now.' She paused. 'Is it easier to be cruel when you're young? Or is it harder?'

Jamie did not answer. Instead, he asked, 'What happened to him? Later? After university?'

'He disappeared into obscurity,' Isabel replied. 'But I did hear that he married an actress. She had parts in radio plays. Then she started appearing in pantomime at the King's Theatre.'

'The trajectory,' mused Jamie. 'And him?'

'He ran a garden centre that belonged to his parents. It sold plants and lawn fertiliser and things like that. I saw him there once, showing a watering can to a customer. I don't think he recognised me.' It occurred to her that it was only too predictable that someone who had always told others what to do should end up showing them how to use a watering can.

Jamie started to dress. 'Oh well, he brought it upon himself. And we've all done things we regret. We're all thoughtless at that stage in our lives.'

'Yes, we are. But it still makes me ashamed just to think about it. We made a joke of his shame – sitting there struggling not to laugh while he had his driving licence suspended and was fined whatever sum it was.'

'Drinking and driving is an offence,' said Jamie. 'He can't complain.'

'No, but we shouldn't have done what we did.'

Jamie thought for a moment. 'Couldn't we all say that about ourselves? As nations, too? *We shouldn't have done what we did.* Isn't that what we all now feel about our past?'

'You mean Britain shouldn't have done what it did? Or America? Or Spain?'

'Yes,' said Jamie. 'But not just them. Not just the obvious targets. Pretty much everybody. Russia. Turkey. China. The past is pretty shameful once you start to look at it more closely.'

Isabel reflected on this as she watched Jamie slip into his clothes. He *slipped* into them, she thought. Others struggled to fit into their clothes, breathed in, pushed and pulled. Jamie slipped.

'I think that we have to be careful,' she said. 'It ties in with what I was saying about being too good. Being too aware of your past can paralyse you.'

This was familiar territory – the drawing of the boundaries of our duty to others – the describing of the circle of our moral concern. We could not assume the full burden of the past: a certain measure of discernment was necessary in distinguishing what we needed to answer for from what could be consigned to history. At some point, thought Isabel, we needed to be able to say, *That was them, not me. That was then, not now.*

Jamie was now combing his hair. 'That new shampoo,' he said.

'Yes.'

'I rather like it. What's it called?'

Isabel told him, and mentioned its risible claims.

'Good choice,' said Jamie, only half seriously. On impulse, he took a few steps – Isabel had been sitting on the edge of the bath – and kissed her. He smelled of the thinking man's shampoo, which had sandalwood in it, she thought – or the chemicals that imitated sandalwood, for so much now was the chemical signature, not the real thing. She thought of truffle flavouring and how the chemists had replaced the dogs used to hunt the wild fungus.

She looked at him. Her hand went to his, and for a moment she held it. Oddly, and for no particular reason, she pictured the mountains of Moidart, a remote and rugged part of the Scottish Highlands. She remembered they had cycled up there once, shortly after they had married, and had stopped by one of those tumbling waterfalls that descend those mountainsides, and are blown by the wind. Jamie had suddenly kissed her – just as he had done a few moments ago – and she'd wondered whether, years later, she might remember the moment; and now she had, two small children later, in a world that was so different from the world of that time, and so much more cynical, too, she thought. Yet Jamie had not changed. He looked exactly the way he looked then; he said the same things; comforted her with the same endearments; thought the same things; loved her, she hoped, in the same way and with exactly the same passion. In all of that, she had been so blessed that she hardly dared contemplate her good fortune. Nemesis lurked – she knew that – scanning her radar screen for those who wandered onto it when she felt in vindictive mood. Only by never manifesting pride in any form could one hope to avoid the unwelcome attention of the goddess. That was clear enough, thought Isabel, even if not always very easy.

Jamie had taken his shower at six-thirty in the evening – a time at which he would normally be involved in the bedtime routine planned for their two small sons, Charlie and Magnus. On this occasion, he and Isabel were preparing to go out to the opening of an exhibition at the Scottish National Portrait Gallery, Isabel's housekeeper, Grace, having been engaged to babysit for the evening. Grace was uncomplaining about this, as she liked watching television from the sofa in the study, where she enjoyed the consumption of salted cashew nuts, smoked oysters on small buttered oatcakes, and quantities of slimline tonic flavoured with slices of lime. There was no reason why such indulgences might not be available in her own flat – other than that she would not buy them.

In addition to the snacks, Jamie always cooked supper for Grace when she was babysitting and left this in the warming oven for her to have whenever she wished. On this particular evening, he had cooked a dish of cauliflower cheese, and had made a mixed salad to accompany it. He knew that this was one of Grace's favourites, and that if a bottle of Chianti were left on the table, Grace would feel that she wanted for nothing. Babysitting was simply an extension of the daycare she provided for Charlie and Magnus on those occasions when Isabel had an editorial task to perform or when she was suddenly called away to a meeting. Grace did not mind any of this and could spend hours with the boys, on whom she appeared to have a particular calming effect. She regularly read to them, affecting a variety of accents to bring out the dramatic quality of whatever book they were enjoying. Isabel had noticed that inevitably, when she read out the villains' dialogue, Grace had them speaking with a Glaswegian accent. She had thought of asking Grace about this, and implying, gently of course, that it might be a bit unfair to stereotype people in this way, but she had refrained from doing so. Grace was sensitive, and might resent any suggestion that she had some sort of prejudice against Glasgow.

Grace arrived in time to give the boys their bath. This was an occasion for shipping accidents, as the boys' fleet of brightly coloured boats, tugs and tankers and fishing vessels, collided with one another in the bathwater or ploughed, like tiny *Titanics*, into icebergs of floating soap. Grace tolerated all this until, precisely ten minutes after bath time had begun, she announced its end and would pull out the plug to forestall any appeal for an extension.

Then it was story time, which that evening was a story set on a Scottish island, the home of a colony of helpful talking seals. The seals were in peril, though, from a visiting shark, whose lines were rendered by Grace in the exaggerated tones of working-class Glasgow. Isabel and Jamie were on the point of leaving at that stage, and exchanged amused glances as they overheard Grace's rendition of the shark's unfriendly threats.

'It's interesting,' said Isabel, as they closed the front door behind them. 'Grace doesn't think of herself as prejudiced, but ...'

Jamie nodded. 'Prejudiced people never do.'

And yet, even as she said this, Isabel thought that to

describe Grace as prejudiced might be a bit unfair. Grace was not intolerant, but she certainly had firm views, and none of the reticence of the middle classes about giving vent to her opinions. If somebody was lazy, Grace would say so, whereas another might be reluctant to use that label. Similarly, if a criminal were sent to prison, Grace might say, 'Well, he asked for that, didn't he?' It might not be that simple for Isabel, who understood how much crime was the product of things over which one had no control.

'A young man who's sent to prison for assault or robbery or whatever it is, ends up there because of what happened before he was born,' she said now, adding, 'At least in part.'

Jamie looked puzzled. He was not sure what had prompted Isabel to make this remark.

'I was just thinking of Grace's views on crime,' she said. 'And that made me think about how crimes are caused by background factors.'

Jamie looked dubious. 'That's a bit determinist, don't you think?'

Isabel defended herself. 'I said *in part*. He – the young man – is in trouble because his father wasn't there when he was a boy. Or his mother was on drugs. Or because of a hundred other things in his background. Of course not everyone who has a bad start like that ends up behaving badly. Obviously, many don't.' She paused. 'There's nothing earth-shattering in that. It's simply moral luck.'

Jamie remembered Isabel talking about this before. 'Of course. Bernard ...' Isabel's philosophers had a tendency to merge into one in Jamie's mind.

'Bernard Williams. Yes, it was his term. And then Thomas Nagel wrote about it. They pointed out what was, I suppose, pretty obvious: that luck plays a major role in determining our fate. They gave the idea a broader intellectual framework.'

Jamie thought about this, and realised that it was hard to argue against the basic premise. It was true: our fate was very largely decided by factors over which we had no real control – parentage and schooling being examples. And yet, that could never be a complete excuse, because if it were, any system of blame and punishment would be defeated. So he simply said, 'Oh well, it's complicated, isn't it?' That was his way of ending a discussion with Isabel – a sort of code – which would result in her saying, 'Yes, very complicated,' and they would move on to another subject altogether. Such codes and shortcuts exist in every marriage – a few words, a gesture, even a slight change in expression, may forfend disagreement and dispute. One friend of theirs simply said *ibi sumus,* pig Latin for 'there we are', when he felt a matter had been adequately aired. And then, of course, there was 'I rest my cake', which was an expression Isabel had been delighted to hear being used by a teenager, unconscious of the malapropism involved. She had then used it herself, as had Jamie, to their private amusement. That, she thought, was the joy of private jokes: they never stopped being funny.

Now they were at the gate and started to walk towards Bruntsfield, where they knew they could pick up a taxi. As they made their way along Merchiston Crescent, Jamie slipped his hand into Isabel's. She took it and pressed it gently – in a gesture of complicity.

'I feel almost irresponsible,' he said. 'Leaving Grace with the boys and going out – just the two of us.'

'Parents have to have some sort of life,' Isabel reassured him. 'And it's not as if we're going out to a nightclub. Or even a bar.'

Jamie laughed. 'I can't remember when I last went to a bar.'

11

'It was last week, actually,' Isabel pointed out. 'You said that you had a drink with that quartet you were playing with. Remember? You said you went to the bar in the Queen's Hall after the rehearsal.'

'Oh, that. That's not really a bar. Well, it is, I suppose, but it's not a pub, if you see what I mean. It's a sort of . . . well, it's a place where musicians . . .'

'Where musicians have a drink,' said Isabel. 'It's a bar, I think.'

Jamie conceded the point. 'And you?'

'I've never been a great enthusiast for bars,' said Isabel. 'As you know. But I did go to the Café Royal a few months ago. You were in Glasgow that day, I seem to recall. The book group I belong to met for its annual lunch there. They invited me, although I've missed four of the last eight meetings. They're very understanding.' She paused, feeling she had to explain. 'The boys, you see. The *Review*. Life . . .'

'The Café Royal doesn't really count,' said Jamie. 'It's like going to a museum or the Vatican Library, or something. Those ornate surroundings.'

'Do you think anybody – a visitor to Rome, a tourist – has ever gone by mistake into the Vatican Library and ordered a drink – or a pizza?'

Jamie smiled. This was typical: Isabel had a tendency to engage in flights of fantasy. 'What?'

'People make mistakes. I just thought that people must wander into the wrong place from time to time. Or get people wrong. They might think that the person they're talking to is somebody else altogether.' She smiled as she remembered a story her mother had told her. 'A cousin of my mother's once mistook General Curtis LeMay for the lift attendant. It was a long time ago. Her husband was a junior economist with

12

the World Bank and she came upon him in the elevator, as they call it in America, and she asked him to take her to the sixth floor.'

Jamie smiled. 'And?'

'And he did. He was very charming about it. And of course he would have been wearing a uniform with a lot of gold braid — exactly the sort of thing a lift attendant might wear.' She remembered something else. 'And what about the current Dutch king? He used to be a qualified airline captain and liked to fly KLM passenger planes. He would sometimes walk down the aisle to greet the passengers and they'd look up and see the Crown Prince. A business-class passenger once asked him to make her a cup of tea. Once again, he was very charming about it — just like General LeMay.'

Jamie said he thought that people who had nothing to prove were usually charming in their dealings with others. 'Only the insecure are nasty,' he said.

'True,' said Isabel, and pressed his hand again, not meaning to do so, but in a moment of pride that she was married to a man who was so completely secure. Jamie never said anything snide or dismissive about anybody else because he had no need to. It was as simple as that.

2

The exhibition at the Scottish National Portrait Gallery on Queen Street had an intriguing title: *Who Were They?* One might expect such a title to be explained by a subtitle, but in this case there was none. The aim of the exhibition, though, was made clear by the paintings selected for the show, the criterion for inclusion being a single quality: the obscurity of the subjects.

'I see what they're getting at,' said Isabel, as she and Jamie began to look at the portraits lining the walls of the gallery. 'All these people are pretty much unknown. Forgotten about.'

Jamie peered at a portrait of a thin-faced middle-aged man wearing a high, uncomfortable collar. He looked at the catalogue they had been given on arrival. 'This one, for instance: we're told he was a fireproof-brick manufacturer who set up a children's home in the late nineteenth century. The children were sent to Canada or Australia to begin a new life.' He paused. 'It says: "Their fate was a mixed one."'

'Child migrants,' said Isabel. 'That went on until not all that long ago.'

Jamie peered at the portrait. 'He's very pleased with himself,' he said.

'If one's fireproof, I suppose . . .' Isabel muttered.

Jamie glanced at her.

'A lot of the children who were sent were used as cheap labour on farms,' Isabel continued. 'They were exploited pretty badly. Others . . . Well, there must have been others for whom it was the best thing that could have happened. Plucked out of the slums of Glasgow or Dundee and given room to breathe on the prairies – there were worse fates.'

Jamie had moved to the next portrait. 'Mrs Anstruther,' he read from the catalogue. 'The widow of Mr Thomas Anstruther of Abergarvie, and the inventor of Mrs Anstruther's Pills, a nineteenth-century patent medicine from which she made a considerable fortune. That fortune was left to a trust for the improvement of miners' housing in West Lothian and Fife.'

'She did the right thing,' said Isabel. 'Although I suspect her pills were powdered chalk, and made no difference. But others were not so benign. They loved putting stuff like arsenic into those remedies.'

Jamie flipped through the catalogue. 'I like the idea of this show,' he said. 'All the people upstairs are well known. The Humes and the Stuarts and the Professor Higgses, and so on. But this place is also full of tucked-away pictures telling a big story.'

'Exactly,' said Isabel. She was now looking at a portrait of a man who had commanded a Scottish regiment in a long-forgotten campaign in a country that had long since ceased to exist. She noticed that in spite of the military uniform, the medals, the officer's sword with its silver handle, the soldier had

15

a weak chin. Perhaps a man with a stronger chin would not have felt the need for all those decorations, might never have felt he needed to be a soldier. The artist seemed to have drawn attention to the chin, which was painted in great detail, and was the point at which the viewer's eye came to rest. Perhaps the artist sensed what I have sensed, thought Isabel – that in this man's chin was his destiny.

'Look at this,' she said, pointing to the military portrait.

Jamie looked, but only briefly. Then he leaned forward and whispered something into Isabel's ear. She felt herself blush. 'Really?' she stuttered.

Jamie nodded. 'Obvious,' he said.

'You don't think you're being a bit uncharitable?'

He smiled. 'Yes, I am. Sorry. Poor guy.'

The crowd had built up. Now a circle opened up around the curator of the exhibition. She handed her glass of wine to an assistant, and began her speech of welcome.

'We thought,' she said, 'of calling this exhibition something like *Lesser-Known Portraits from the Collection*, but realised, once we started to put it together, that such a title would be misleading. These are not lesser-known portraits – these are completely forgotten portraits. But that does not mean that they no longer speak to us, sometimes quite eloquently, of their particular times. So, we chose *Who Were They?* instead.'

The speech did not last long, and the milling-about continued. Isabel and Jamie became detached from one another when he stopped to talk to somebody he knew, and she found herself standing in front of a small portrait of a footballer of the 1930s. It was not a particularly good portrait, she thought, and was about to move on when the curator, Andrea Clement, appeared at her side. Isabel knew her slightly from the meetings of the Cockburn Society, an architectural conservation body of which they were both members.

'Approve of it?' asked Andrea, gesturing to the walls of paintings.

'Very much,' said Isabel. 'It's a great idea. Another example of the history-from-the-bottom-up approach.'

'That's what we thought,' said Andrea. She paused. 'I was hoping to have a word with you, actually. I saw your name on the invitations list. And thank you, by the way, for your support.' Isabel was a member of the gallery's patron scheme.

'I've always liked this place,' said Isabel.

'That's why I thought I might ask you,' said Andrea.

Isabel waited.

'We're creating an advisory board,' Andrea explained. 'It's a fairly informal set-up. Its purpose is to keep us in touch with what people would like us to do.'

'A sort of users' panel?'

'You could call it that. The advisory board will be quite distinct from the formal governing board – the trustees – and it won't have any actual responsibilities. I suppose you might call it a sounding board, or a focus group. I don't much like the term *focus group* myself, but we all know what such groups do. Advise. Encourage. Respond to ideas. Warn if they think we're going down the wrong track.'

Isabel hesitated. She glanced across the room to where Jamie was still standing, talking to his friend. Jamie was always concerned about her taking on further responsibilities. 'You have more than enough in your life,' he had said a couple of weeks earlier when she had raised the possibility of going on a committee that had approached her. 'Do you need to take this on? Do you really need to be on this?'

She had declined the invitation, and yet here was another

one. This one, though, was for something in which she had a strong interest. This would not be work, as such. This one . . . She imagined the excuses she could give Jamie, and then thought, no, it was *her* time, not his, and even if he was right in saying that she could never turn things down, she was still entitled to do the things that appealed to her.

'You might want some time to think it over,' said Andrea 'I hope you'll say yes, but you might want to discuss it with your husband.' Andrea glanced over towards Jamie.

Isabel frowned. Why would Andrea think she needed to do that?

'No,' she said. 'I don't need to think it over. I rather like the sound of it.'

Andrea looked pleased. 'You'll accept?'

'With pleasure,' said Isabel.

They stayed for less than an hour at the gallery. That gave them sufficient time to look at all thirty portraits in the exhibition and to have enough conversations to want to get out into the fresh air. The opening of an exhibition, Isabel had always thought, was not all that different from a cocktail party, and made the same demands on one's feet and one's capacity for small talk. That evening, she and Jamie had been separated at an early stage, and by the time they met again, in front of the beaming portrait of a nineteenth-century brewer, who was bedecked in tartan and sporting a clan chief's feathers – to which he would not have been entitled – Isabel was ready to leave.

'I think we should slip away in ten minutes or so,' she whispered. 'I'd like to have dinner.'

Jamie agreed readily. 'I was stuck for twenty minutes with that woman over there . . . you know the one.' He inclined his head in the direction of a woman in a red silk shift. 'I couldn't get away. I tried, but she kept grabbing my arm and saying how much she liked the bassoon.'

Isabel had seen it. She knew the woman. She always made eyes at Jamie – there was nothing unusual about that. Jamie's attractiveness rarely went unnoticed, although he often failed to realise that he was the object of appreciative glances. That evening, though, he was being *pawed*; there was no other word for it. She grinned. 'I was going to come to your rescue, but I was caught myself. Somebody was showing me his new Apple watch. Can you believe it? One comes to the opening of an important exhibition and you find yourself talking to somebody who's keen to demonstrate what his new Apple watch can do.'

Jamie laughed. 'There are geeks everywhere. But now they're no longer ashamed of themselves. They've come out. You were fortunate – he might have been a radio ham. My father had a cousin who talked about nothing but amateur radio. It was his absolute passion. He was always going on about wavelengths and antennae. I even remember some of the things he told me when I was a boy.'

'Such as?'

'Oh, the way in which the ionosphere enables you to bounce signals off it. You can send signals all the way round the world like that. But only High Frequency. Not VHF or UHF.' He paused, and gave Isabel a serious look. 'There's a difference, you know. High Frequency signals go between 3 and 30 megahertz. Very High Frequency signals are between ... no, don't tell me, I can actually remember ... between 30 and 300 megahertz. Yes, that's right. Don't try and bounce those off the ionosphere – it won't work.'

'I don't believe it!' exclaimed Isabel. 'You've remembered *that*?'

'I have,' said Jamie, a little proudly. And then added, 'Actually, I not only remember some of that stuff, but he also used to talk to me about human hearing. He knew of my passion for music and he thought I might be interested – which I was, I suppose.'

Isabel was still holding her largely untouched glass of wine. She now took a sip, and waited.

'Human hearing, then?' said Jamie. '20 hertz to 20 kilohertz. Low to high. Babies can probably hear sounds a bit higher than that. Cats go up to 60 kilohertz. Dogs, I think, manage about 40, which is not quite so high.'

'Oh.' Isabel thought of Brother Fox, whom they saw in their garden, who sometimes seemed to be disturbed by things that she could not hear. Of course, he was more dog than cat, so his ears would not be so sensitive. She had always thought, though, that Brother Fox had some form of extra-sensory perception, and that, she imagined, would be unmeasurable in terms of these kilohertz that Jamie was talking about. Brother Fox *knew* things that humans did not know. If there were things of which we were blissfully ignorant, then Brother Fox probably had wind of them well before the event.

'Rock musicians,' Jamie remarked. 'They're another case altogether. There was something in the Musicians' Union magazine about them. Industrial injury issues. Apparently, the Swedes have been doing research on hearing problems in rock musicians, and almost half of them have impaired hearing – at both ends of the scale – both low and high sounds.'

'Self-inflicted, though,' said Isabel. 'They don't *have* to be so loud.'

'Perhaps,' said Jamie. 'But rock *is* loud. If it's not loud, it's not rock.'

Isabel did not particularly like rock music. Apart from

Creedence Clearwater Revival, of course, and she thought of another band, who were very loud as she recalled, but whose music, or name, she could not remember. She remembered that she had liked them, though. Jamie would know who they were if she could only find some way of describing them, but she could not even remember what they looked like, or where they came from. They were not Swedish, she thought.

They left discreetly. Outside, on Queen Street, it was still light, and the air was warm. It was September, and the days were starting to shorten. In these latitudes – Edinburgh lay at 55 degrees, although a drift of less than 4,000 feet would make it 56 degrees – at these latitudes it barely became dark at midnight. Now, at half past eight, the evening sun was still on the rooftop, still bathing the stone of the buildings with gold. Night seemed to be no issue, and time seemed abundant, almost limitless. There was no urgency in a northern summer, because each day so easily and painlessly became the next day, and the day after that.

A tram rumbled past. A man and a woman, seated at the front, gazed out of the window as the tram gathered speed to climb up to St Andrew Square. He was wearing a grey overcoat and a brown fedora; she had a pill-box hat and a dark green jacket. There was something strikingly old-fashioned about them, and Isabel touched Jamie's arm to draw his attention.

'Those people,' she said. 'Look. They're straight out of an Edward Hopper painting.'

Jamie turned, and the couple intercepted his and Isabel's stares. Then, just before they drew out of sight, the man smiled and raised his hat. The woman looked in their direction and smiled too. Then they were gone.

'They were,' said Isabel. 'They really were. They were

people from a painting by Hopper. That's what people looked like in his pictures. They looked lonely.'

Jamie gazed after the departing tram. 'They were with each other,' he said.

'Yes,' she said. 'They were. But it was the way they were dressed. The colour of his coat. Her jacket. Her hat. They were Hopper clothes.'

Jamie looked at his watch. 'Where are we going to have dinner?'

Isabel shrugged. 'There are plenty of places.'

'I think we're walking in the wrong direction. We need to be going west, not east.'

They turned round and retraced their steps back along Queen Street. A few blocks later, they found a small Italian restaurant that would take them without a reservation, and they were shown to their table.

Jamie glanced at the menu briefly before handing it to Isabel. 'You choose. I don't care what I have.'

She made their choice. 'Italian comfort food,' she said. 'Caprese salad. Spaghetti carbonara. A red wine from Puglia.'

'Perfect,' said Jamie. 'That's all we need, really.'

'And some focaccia to dip into olive oil.'

'Heaven,' said Jamie. He looked at her, as if he wanted her to agree with what he was about to say. 'Do you think we're lucky?' he asked.

She was slightly taken aback by the question. But there could only be one answer to that, in her view. 'Very lucky,' she said.

He smiled. 'Do you remember the scene in *Casablanca* where everybody in Rick's sings "Knock on Wood"? Remember that?'

She did. And she remembered the words. 'The singer asks who's lucky, and everybody sings "We're all lucky" and then

22

they all knock on wood.' She laughed. 'I love that scene. Everybody was so high-spirited.'

'And when they played "La Marseillaise" in Rick's, everybody stood up and sang . . . '

'And the extras in the film – the people doing the singing – were *real* exiles, washed up in Hollywood because of the war in Europe, and they meant every word, and they were in tears. That's a little detail, I know, but I've always remembered that.'

'We must watch it again,' said Jamie. 'You and me. I could make some cheese straws, and we could watch it on the sofa, after the boys have gone to bed.'

She closed her eyes. She was immensely lucky. Immensely. But then she said, 'But why do you ask?'

He shrugged. 'Because people often don't realise how lucky they are.'

'No?'

Jamie warmed to his theme. 'No. Even if they don't look particularly lucky from the outside, so to speak. They may still be extremely lucky – just to be alive. That's luck enough, I would have thought. And then, to be living now, at our stage in history, rather than before modern dentistry, and anaesthetics, or the Universal Declaration of Human Rights, for that matter. And here, rather than in the middle of a war zone somewhere. There are so many grounds for considering oneself fortunate. You hardly have to look.'

She agreed you did not.

The waiter came to take their order. Within a couple of minutes he was back with the wine, which he served with a flourish. He was from Puglia, he said, and he was proud of this wine. His uncle knew the man who made it.

Jamie raised his glass to Isabel. 'You were talking to that curator person,' he said. 'What's her name again?'

'Andrea. Andrea Clement. I knew somebody called Clement once. I don't know if they're connected. They could be. She — the Clement I knew — was a serious basketball player. She had a boyfriend who played rugby for Scotland. He was really tall. Massive. Mind you, she was tall too — hence the basketball.'

Jamie brushed aside the irrelevant detail. Such things could waylay any conversation in Scotland — some link between people. Everybody, it seemed, was linked in some way, and it could be distracting. 'Yes, her. The person who made the speech. What were you talking about?'

Isabel hesitated. 'The Portrait Gallery,' she said. 'Their plans.'

Jamie was looking at her with interest. 'And do those plans affect you?'

She frowned. 'Affect me?' She could feel her neck getting warmer. It did that when she felt awkward or embarrassed.

'Isabel . . . ' There was a tone of reproach in his voice.

She looked at him, trying not to smile. 'I wish I could hide things from you, but I can't.'

'And I can't hide things from you either.'

She thought about what she had just said. 'Actually, I *don't* wish I could hide things from you. I don't know why I said that. I can't imagine what it must be like to be in a marriage in which there were secrets.'

That interested Jamie. He had always imagined that all marriages had at least some secrets, even if small and incon-sequential ones. Or were people franker than he imagined, confessing absolutely everything to their partner? 'Everybody,' he said, hesitantly, 'has at least something he keeps from those who are close to him. Some secret thoughts, for instance.'

She looked at him across the table. 'Fantasies, you mean?'

He looked away. 'Perhaps.'

Isabel had started this conversation, but now she was not

sure that she wanted to continue with it. Did Jamie *think* about other women, even if she knew, was as certain as she possibly could be, that he would never be unfaithful to her in the flesh. Did he imagine things, as she had read somewhere all men did? She tried not to think about it, because the thought was so unsettling. And yet, did it matter? The human mind was capable of an astonishing degree of compartmentalisation: private thoughts, never acted upon, were no threat in the real world of action and feeling.

She almost asked him, there and then, but stopped herself. She almost said, 'Jamie, do you ever dream of other women? Just dream?'

Of course she did not mean dream. She meant fantasise: dreams were another matter altogether. We had no control over our dreams because they *happened* to us. Nobody could be blamed for what he or she dreamed, unless . . . She began to imagine a moral basis for the accountability of the dreamer. Perhaps she might even invite somebody to write a paper on it for the *Review*, in which they would examine whether we might be responsible for the state of our subconscious minds. The argument would be quite straightforward: if you allowed your mind to dwell on certain matters – if you gave those matters *mental room* – then you might be responsible for the impact of those ideas on your subconscious. That raised the issue of disposition, or character, she thought. A familiar argument against screen violence was that it corrupted the disposition of those exposed to it. And a malignant disposition could – just could – manifest itself in vicious action at some point. In this way, private mental activity, apparently harmless to others, became a threat. If you allowed yourself to fantasise about hurting others – and enjoying it – then some day you might translate your thoughts into action. The police would

25

confirm that, she suspected. When they searched the homes of those suspected of violent crimes, they sometimes found caches of disturbing material – images of exactly the sort of act that had then been committed – the inspiration, so to speak, for what had been done. *Post hoc, ergo propter hoc*: after this, therefore because of this. It was enticing reasoning – a philosophical siren – one of those phrases that provided a persuasive intellectual shortcut, but which needed to be handled carefully.

Of course, none of this was new. The state of the subconscious and the state of the soul were probably one and the same thing, the only real difference being the language used. In the past, people wrestled with demons; now they struggled with attitudes and urges. Was there all that much difference?

The waiter brought their first course, their Caprese salad, and thoughts of the subconscious were replaced by thoughts of mozzarella – which was probably for the best, thought Isabel, because she and Jamie were out for dinner together and she did not want to get bogged down in a debate on the cultivation of character. Jamie was interested in philosophy, increasingly so with each year of marriage to Isabel, but he would not necessarily want to talk about it on their night out, over an Italian meal, with 'Return to Sorrento' playing softly, somewhere in the background.

He had noticed it, of course, as musicians do. Most of us are indifferent to background music in restaurants, as long as it doesn't impede conversation; we ignore it, just as we ignore traffic noise or the hum of the refrigerator. Piped music is like wallpaper now; one accepts it, even if it isn't to one's taste. The battle for silence in public spaces had long been lost, Isabel believed.

But now Jamie looked up from his mozzarella and

26

tomatoes and said, 'If Italian restaurants are to be believed, they never seem to get back to Sorrento. They think about returning. They sing about it. But do they ever actually get back?'

Isabel laughed. 'It's the same with songs about Skye,' she said. 'I think of them in their little boat, heading across the Minch, caught forever by song between South Uist and Skye. Or that song – "The Road to the Isles" that Kenneth McKellar would sing with such utter conviction. I see him striding along, cromach in hand, being called by the distant Cuillins, but never actually reaching the end of the Road to the Isles.' She paused. 'Which I suppose is now called the A95.'

'Music captures a moment,' said Jamie. 'It exists in a realm of time and place that isn't necessarily the same as the one we live in. You do know that, don't you?' He did not wait for Isabel to answer, but returned to the question he had asked earlier, about her conversation with Andrea.

'She's asked you to do something, hasn't she?'

Isabel speared a slice of tomato. The olive oil glistened on it – little drops of green. A milky streak, the liquid from the mozzarella, intersected the tomato, like lines on a map. She said, 'She did, as it happens.'

'And you accepted?'

She nodded. 'I know you think I'm incapable of saying no to people. That's what you always say.'

Obligingly, Jamie said, 'You're incapable of saying no to people, Isabel.'

'Well, in this case, it's not a big thing. An advisory committee.' She took a mouthful of tomato and mozzarella before continuing, 'I don't think it will involve much. She said there would be a meeting every three months or so. That's hardly onerous.'

Jamie agreed that it did not sound like much. 'But I'll tell you what will happen. Do you want to hear?'

'I don't believe I have much choice.'

'Something will crop up. Somebody on the committee will draw you into something. And you'll be too soft-hearted, too kind to say, "Look, this isn't my business." That's what you *should* say, you know.'

He looked at her and sighed. 'And I've told you before, so here goes again: if that's the way it has to be for you, then that's the way it has to be. But I'm not going to be surprised when it happens exactly as I've said it'll happen.'

'Let's talk about Puglia instead,' said Isabel.

Jamie's face broke into a smile. He reached out and touched her hand. 'Of course. Shall we go there one day? Soon?'

'Yes.'

Jamie took a sip of wine. 'We'll rent a house – one of those white-washed houses on the brow of a hill, with ancient olive groves around it.'

'And the sound of cicadas . . . '

'And there'll be a hammock for you to read in,' Jamie said. 'While I take the boys for a walk down a road with white dust and we'll pick wild flowers for you, me and the boys, and at night the sky will be studded with stars, and we'll sit out in front of the house, hoping to feel a cool breeze . . . '

Isabel smiled. 'And the sound of cicadas will still be there.'

'Yes, it will.'

She remembered Carlo Levi. '*Cristo si è fermato a Eboli,*' she muttered.

He looked at her quizzically.

'"Christ stopped at Eboli",' she explained. 'Carlo Levi's book. He was exiled to that part of Italy in the 1930s. He describes it so well. The desperation, the feeling that the people down there had of having been bypassed by everything. And there's a marching band in it. It marches over a cliff, but can still be heard playing. A ghost band.'

Jamie said nothing, and so Isabel added, 'In Italy, you get the feeling that magic realism is actually realism. There's no distinction.'

'Oh,' said Jamie. He loved Italy. There was nothing about it he did not like – except the politics, and the bad driving, and the incorrigibility of the south. That left art, and cuisine, and laughter, and the sense of style. Was it not possible to have northern moral seriousness and Italian warmth combined? He thought it was, although he had once asked Isabel that precise question, and she had shaken her head. Impossible, she said. Moral seriousness requires a very different climate: mists, cold, a Reformation. He wondered whether she was being ironical – there was a hint of a smile about her lips as she spoke, which pointed in that direction.

They decided to walk back, rather than look for a taxi or take a bus. There was no hurry to relieve Grace, as she often stayed the night when she babysat, and had offered to do so on this occasion. It took them an hour and a half, as they stopped on the way for a cup of coffee from a coffee stall on the edge of the Meadows. The night was still warm, and there were still people out and about in the encroaching gloaming, such as it was at Edinburgh's latitude, some of them sprawled out on the grass. Two dogs chased one another, yapping shrilly, ignoring their owners' calls, determined to make the most of the day's embers; somebody was playing a radio; a young woman nearby, standing under a tree with her boyfriend, began to sob.

'That's the end of that relationship,' muttered Jamie.

Isabel glanced at the couple. They were too self-absorbed to care very much that others might see them, but she still looked away quickly, in case they noticed. 'Poor girl,' she said. 'He's ending it – obviously.'

Jamie smiled. That was the woman's view of the situation, he thought – an assumption of male fault. 'Or she's found out he's been seeing somebody else,' he suggested.

Isabel considered this possibility briefly. 'Possibly,' she said. 'Although if that were the case, she might be angry rather than sad.' She paused. 'I wonder if anybody's done any research as to whether more relationships are ended by men than by women. What do you think?'

'Everything has been researched,' said Jamie. 'There are very few stones left unturned.'

'It would also be interesting to find out whether women think that men break up with them more frequently than they break up with men – if you see what I mean.'

'Whether women think men are usually to blame? Or less faithful?'

'Yes,' said Isabel.

Jamie shrugged. He noticed that the boy had now left the young woman standing under the tree, and was strolling off, back towards George Square and the University Library, which was still ablaze with light for the studious few. 'Look,' he said. 'He's walked off.'

Isabel stopped. She saw that the young woman's head was lowered. Even at that distance, she was a picture of misery.

'Look at her,' said Isabel, her voice lowered in sympathy, although they were well out of earshot. 'We can't leave her there. She looks so miserable.'

Jamie had not expected this. 'You mean . . . '

'I mean we should go and ask her if she's all right.'

Jamie drew a deep breath. 'But it's a lovers' tiff,' he protested. 'These things happen all the time. You can't just barge in.'

'I'm not going to barge in,' answered Isabel. 'I just want to see that she's all right.' She looked at Jamie. 'If you were crying under a tree, wouldn't you be comforted if somebody stopped and had a word with you?'

He thought about this. She was right. And yet, this was just another example of Isabel's feeling that she had to take on the problems of the world, and the world was simply too full of pain and unhappiness for it to be assuaged in this way. A whole lake of suffering, that was how the world might be described – *was* described and tackling it in this way was to take a teaspoon to that lake when what was required was major civil engineering – seismic change, floodgates, great shore defences. And yet, if everybody had their teaspoon with them, and wielded it when that pain and unhappiness came within their view, then it would make a difference and the level of the lake would drop perceptibly. A few small acts of kindness, performed for those in one's immediate vicinity, might not change the overall picture, but when hundreds of people, and then thousands, and then multitudes, did the same, it would be very different. Of course it would.

He nudged her. 'You go. It might be better if it were just you.'

She thought so too, and began to make her way towards the young woman and her tree. Jamie watched. When the young woman looked up in surprise, Isabel reached out and touched her forearm. The young woman responded. She put her hands behind her neck in a gesture that he found hard to interpret. Coming to, one might call it; regaining control of oneself. A *what have I been doing?* gesture.

They spoke for a few minutes. Then they separated, the

31

young woman heading up Middle Meadow Walk while Isabel returned to Jamie.

'She's all right,' she said. 'She's going back to her flat. They're students.'

'I thought they might be,' said Jamie. 'And?'

Isabel took his arm as they continued their walk home. 'She'd just ditched him.'

'She did?' exclaimed Jamie.

'Yes,' Isabel continued. 'She said that she had told him it was over. He was very upset, apparently. She said he was a nice boy. A medical student. From Carnoustie.'

Jamie showed his surprise. 'But what's that got to do with it? The fact that he's from Carnoustie. Of all places.' He had always been impressed by Isabel's ability to ferret out personal or social detail from the briefest of encounters.

'I asked her,' she replied. 'At first glance it has nothing to do with it, but then, on the other hand, Carnoustie is just the sort of place in which you'd expect to find decent, respectable boys – like her ex.' She smiled. 'I asked her because it helps me to understand the situation.'

'Which is?'

Isabel thought for a few moments before making her diagnosis. 'Shall I paraphrase? She's an attractive girl. She's twenty, and enjoying the freedom of university. She meets a clean-cut medical student – from Carnoustie. She encourages him but she soon becomes bored. Perhaps she meets a good-looking American student on a year abroad exchange – from somewhere like Dartmouth College. Her head's turned. She realises that the medical student from Carnoustie is a bit dull. The boy-next-door issue. And that's the end of the affair.'

Jamie was wide-eyed. Of course; of course. It all made sense, and he could just – just – believe Isabel's fantasy. And yet . . .

32

'She was the one in tears,' he pointed out. 'But you say that she had done the ditching. Is that right?'

'Yes,' said Isabel, her tone slightly sheepish. She had been so wrong. 'She said that she found the split-up just too emotional, even if she was relieved that it was coming to an end.'

Jamie was not sure what to say. Perhaps the young woman had felt guilt; guilt was quite capable of bringing on tears. And of course anyone might feel guilty about being unkind to a boy from Carnoustie. It was a place of well-set small villas and golf courses, braced against the invigorating breezes of the North Sea, a town that embodied the values of Middle Scotland, just as Muncie, Indiana, did the same thing for Middle America. No, one should not be unkind to those who came from Carnoustie . . .

'Anyway,' Isabel continued, 'I'm glad I went to speak to her, even if I didn't get it right.'

Jamie laughed. But he still said, 'I'm proud of you.' And he was: he knew plenty of people who would have paid no attention to that young woman's tears. Isabel was not one of them.

Isabel did not respond to the compliment, but she was pleased, and she leaned against him briefly as they walked; two lovers walking home, happy in the way in which homeward-bound lovers tend to be.

3

Isabel had intended to devote the following morning to mundane editorial correspondence – letters
she knew she had to write but that she had been putting off
because they involved some sort of rejection – not a task that
she had ever relished. There were notes to publishers who had
sent her review copies of books, along with fulsome praise
for authors and their work. The space available for reviews
in the *Review of Applied Ethics* was limited – a dozen pages, at
the most, in each issue – and the prolixity of reviewers meant
that no more than six books could be reviewed. Those not
given a full review could be squeezed into a feature entitled
'Briefly Noted', but it was scant consolation for an author,
or a publisher, if a book had no more than a single-sentence
description. Of course, the briefest of reviews could speak vol-
umes: Professor Robert Lettuce, the professor of philosophy
with whom Isabel had been obliged to work from time to time
and for whom she did not have particular regard, was a master
of the succinct put-down, and had used the one line available

to him to denigrate the books of rivals. *Yet another book from Professor Thomas,* he had once written of a colleague's magisterial tome on David Hume. Those who read this and knew that Professor Thomas had consistently written the books that Professor Lettuce himself would have liked to write, had no difficulty in discerning the animus in this brief remark. And then there had been his comment, *This is another book to place on your shelves.* That could be read as an encouragement to buy the book in question, or equally well as an invitation to place the book – unread – on the shelf.

Isabel had a policy of writing to every publisher who sent a review copy and explaining, if the book was not to get a full review, how this decision was based on space considerations rather than on any demerits of the book itself. It would have been easy to write a standard brush-off, or even to ignore, as most editors did, the avalanche of books that made its way onto their desks. But Isabel could not do that, and so each submission was acknowledged and accompanied, if there was to be no review, with a note of regret. 'In an ideal world I would love to publish a review of this title, but considerations of space prevent it.' It was scant comfort for the unreviewed, of course, but it was infinitely better than silence. She understood, in a way that many journal editors did not, how much of an author's life may be invested in a single, obscure tome, and how much publishers shared in the emotional commitment involved in bringing a book into the world. The least she could do, she felt, was to explain why more could not be done to support their venture. Of course, so many academic books were simply not read at all, being so specialised and obscure as to appeal only to a handful of possible readers. Even then, that small coterie of people might simply be too busy to wade through yet another contribution to their tiny field.

She sighed. The world was full of disappointments of every type. Not only were there those whose books would never be reviewed, nor read, there were those who would never write the book they desperately wanted to write – and those, of course, who had written their book but could find nobody to publish it. And then she thought of the songwriters whose songs would never be sung, and the composers whose music would never be played, and the young people who wanted to be doctors but were turned down by medical schools, and the missionaries who found nobody to convert ... The sigh became a smile, as she remembered reading of a Canadian composer who had written a four-act, three-hour opera on the life of a Manitoba dentist and who had bemoaned the failure of Canadian opera companies to perform his work. 'I despair of our cultural policy,' he was quoted as saying. 'If our own opera companies will not perform Canadian work, then music in this country will wither on the vine.'

Of course, it was easy to condescend to dentists. Their work was hardly glamorous, and the life of a Manitoba dentist may seem to be without the kind of incident that an operatic libretto may require, and yet dentists were heroes and heroines, every one of them, in doing what they did for others. A single dentist, Isabel now thought, is worth twenty hedge fund managers ... no, one hundred hedge fund managers, and yet the world did not recognise this incontrovertible fact. Hedge fund managers made millions through what amounted to no more than gambling; dentists could do well, but earned, and were morally entitled to, every penny they made. They brought relief and comfort; hedge fund managers might be necessary for the working of the financial system, but did they deserve those unfathomable profits? Isabel thought not. Croesus could never fully justify his wealth.

36

Now, seated at her desk, with the light of the summer morning casting a buttery yellow square on the carpet, Isabel worked without interruption for several hours. Her list, tackled with such determination, quickly shrank, and now there was only a single review copy to be acknowledged. She opened it, failing to read the author's name on the cover, which featured the image of Poussin's *A Dance to the Music of Time*. The letter inside soon sent her back to the cover, to see the authorial name she had missed. 'Dear Ms Dalhousie,' it began. 'I am sure you will be as pleased to see this book as we are to have published it. Dr Christopher Dove, with whose work you will no doubt be familiar, here turns his formidable talent to an analysis of moral generosity and the role that it plays in our public and private lives. "This astonishingly brilliant book", writes Professor Anthony Salt, "will transform our notions of the impulses and beliefs that lead us to act over and above the call of duty. This book is an essential purchase for every philosophical library, public and private." Strong praise indeed, but very much reflecting our own evaluation of this significant publishing event.'

Isabel frowned. She knew who Professor Anthony Salt was. And she knew, too, that he and Dove were close friends, and had travelled in Morocco together as undergraduates. Christopher Dove himself had once told her about that trip and how he had ransomed Salt from a gang of small-time, bargain-basement kidnappers who preyed on Western backpackers in Marrakech. The kidnappers set their sights low, as a small demand would always be paid promptly and with little fuss. Dove had obtained his friend's release on payment of 200 US dollars – a price that the police, to whom the incident was reported, felt was perhaps on the excessive side – for a philosopher. 'Salt owes me,' Dove had said jokingly. And here, thought Isabel, was Salt repaying him with his gushing recommendation. The book might have its merits, but she wondered whether Anthony Salt really believed what he wrote about it. And what was the precise meaning of the phrase *astonishingly brilliant*? Was Salt astonished that Dove had written something brilliant? If that were so, then the compliment seemed backhanded, which surely could not have been intentional. But, more than that, there was the point that the close relationship between the two meant that Salt could hardly be objective about Dove's work. If somebody saved you from the attentions of Moroccan kidnappers, then you could hardly say that their book was not up to scratch. It might have been better, she thought, had Salt confessed an interest and recused himself from writing the recommendation.

It was some months since Christopher Dove had crossed her mind, and now here he was, talking about moral generosity of all things. What did Dove know about moral generosity? she asked herself. Dove, who was one of the most calculating men she had ever encountered, of whom it was said that he had never knowingly helped anybody or done anything that did not bring him immediate reward in the shape of an invitation to a conference or a comfortable visiting fellowship at a well-endowed university; the very same Dove whom people accused of exploiting post-doctoral research students by getting them to do his research and then failing to acknowledge their contribution; *that* Dove was now lecturing others about how to behave. She put down the book. It was a thick volume – at least 400 pages, she thought. She sighed. She could ignore this book; she could write it off, unread, on the grounds of authorial hypocrisy, but then she stopped herself. The person and the message were *not* the same thing: what was important was what a work said.

She looked out of her window, past the rhododendron bushes under which Brother Fox rested on his silent patrols of the neighbourhood, and within which he might, at that very moment, be concealed in shadow. She was remembering an exchange she had had recently with her friend, Edward Mendelson, in New York, who had written to her about building work he was having done on his house in Maine, but who had somehow drifted off into an examination of Auden's views on how the private life of the poet should not affect our reading of his work. She had agreed with the sentiment, but had remembered that Auden had suppressed one – if not more – of his own poems on the grounds that it was insincere. Of course, that was different: Auden meant that the poem itself should be honest; he had not suggested that a dishonest poet could not write an honest poem. He was right about that, she thought; she did not feel an author's work should be dismissed – or, worse still, proscribed – because of some personal failing. That would cut a swathe through literature. Evelyn Waugh was cantankerous and at times deliberately unpleasant; Patrick O'Brian was egregiously dishonest about his past; Philip Larkin held dismissive views of others; and yet the *Sword of Honour* trilogy was a work of grave beauty; the *Master and Commander* series included some of the finest historical novels in the English language; and 'The Whitsun Weddings' was one of the most memorable poems of its time. A moment's thought brought another example: Patricia Highsmith, whose novels Isabel enjoyed, even after reading a devastating biography of the misanthropic Highsmith – who excoriated many others, appeared to be anti-Semitic, anti-French, anti-everybody, it seemed, and delighted in the predatory destruction of the relationships of others. Patricia Highsmith took simple nastiness to new heights, if her latest biographer was to be believed.

Yet she wrote compelling psychological thrillers that could continue to be enjoyed even if one knew that a poisonous disposition lay behind them. When it came to composers, the issue was exactly the same, as Jamie had pointed out. 'Wagner was dreadful,' he said. 'And yet when it came to writing Wagner, he was unbeatable.' Isabel had laughed. But then Jamie continued, 'And there were plenty of other composers who were less than perfect in their private lives.' There were, she agreed, but should those issues affect our enjoyment of their music? Jamie was not sure. A bad man can cook a good dinner, he reminded himself – and you don't have to eat the dinner *with* him.

She picked up the letter from Christopher Dove's publisher and began to draft a letter. 'Dear Ms Ramsey,' she wrote. 'Thank you for sending me this interesting new book by Christopher Dove. I have not yet had time to read it, but I shall be passing it on to one of our reviewers for a full review. I trust that you will be pleased with that. Yours sincerely, Isabel Dalhousie.'

She looked out of the window again. *Yours sincerely* . . . This letter was anything but. I am trying to do the right thing, she told herself, and I should feel better within myself for overcoming petty resentments. But do I? I don't think I do.

It was the right moment to get up from her desk. She had achieved what she'd set out to achieve and thought that she might now go out for lunch. She would not meet anybody, but would treat herself to a quiet lunch in Bruntsfield, perhaps with the *Scotsman* crossword for company, or an anthology of Arthur Waley's translations of poetry of the Tang dynasty. There was something comforting about reading the musings of exiled Chinese poets while tackling a Caprese salad with a side dish of large green olives.

That was not to be. The Caprese salad materialised, as did the dish of olives, but so did a woman who, seeing Isabel at her table, picked up her bowl of carrot and coriander soup and came over to speak to her.

'I know I shouldn't disturb your lunch,' the woman said, 'but you're Isabel Dalhousie, aren't you, and I believe you and I are going to be seeing a fair amount of one another in the future.'

Isabel looked at her blankly. She wondered whether she should say, 'You're right, I was hoping to have a quiet lunch,' but she did not. Instead, she smiled, and gestured to the empty chair opposite her. 'Please,' she said.

The woman sat down. 'The National Portrait Gallery? I'm the convenor of the committee that you—'

Isabel remembered. 'Of course,' she said.

'I'm Laura Douglas,' said the woman.

Isabel waited.

'I'm so glad you're joining us,' said Laura. 'You see, the committee has only just been set up and already . . . ' She spread her hands in a gesture of resignation.

Isabel sighed. 'Committees,' she said. 'Was there ever a committee that was straightforward?'

Laura seemed pleased with this. 'I'm so glad you understand.'

'Well, I'm not sure—' Isabel began.

Laura interrupted her. 'I'm the chair, you see. I don't know how it happened, but they chose me at the first meeting. I accepted, of course, but I fear that there are one or two members who might have been a bit unhappy with this – one in particular.'

Isabel smiled. 'Let me guess. That's the person who wanted to become chair himself – or herself. Am I right?'

Laura visibly relaxed. 'Absolutely right. He obviously felt

that he should be in the chair. He went so far as to canvas some of the members after that first meeting. He suggested that we might have a special meeting to elect a new chair. One of them came to me and told me all about it. She was really offended, and I think she may have told him so.'

'Well, now he'll know.'

'Yes. She said that in her opinion, he simply wasn't accepting that a woman should be in the chair. She said she could tell that he was one of those men who just won't accept a woman's authority.' She paused. 'There are some like that – still.'

Isabel agreed. 'Fewer and fewer, I think, but they still put their heads above the parapet from time to time.' She speared a tomato stained with mozzarella. 'Who was this . . . this reactionary?'

'A professor of something or other. Philosophy, I think.'

Isabel looked up sharply. The small piece of tomato she had manoeuvred onto her fork fell off, landing on the cuff of her jacket.

'Oh dear,' said Laura. 'Here, let me.' She reached across with her paper napkin and dabbed at the tomato, spreading it rather than retrieving it. 'Oh dear,' she said again.

Isabel used her own napkin to remove the scrap. 'Don't worry. What do they say? Many a slip twixt plate and lip . . . ' She looked at Laura. 'Tell me more about this man. What's his name?'

Laura's eyes lit up mischievously. 'You'd never guess,' she replied. 'It's so ridiculous – and yet somehow it suits him.'

Isabel savoured the moment briefly. 'Professor Lettuce?'

Laura gasped. 'You know him?'

'I do,' said Isabel quietly. 'Robert Lettuce and I go back a long way. We've been on editorial boards together. And other committees from time to time. I've seen him in operation.'

Laura was apologetic. 'Of course. I should have thought of

that. I read that you edited a philosophical journal. Of course you must know him.' A look of anxiety came over her. 'I hope I haven't put my foot in it,' adding, 'yet again.'

Isabel reassured her. There was something about her uninvited lunch companion that appealed to her – an openness. 'Not in the slightest,' she said. 'He and I have crossed swords, or salad forks, perhaps, on a number of occasions before.'

'What would you think if he became convenor?' asked Laura. And then added, 'There – I've put my cards on the table.'

Isabel hesitated. It seemed to her that there was no escape from a looming alliance. She had yet to attend a meeting of this new committee, and already she was *parti pris*.

'I wouldn't necessarily welcome it,' she said at last.

Laura clapped her hands together. 'Oh, wonderful. Nor would I. Nor would . . . ' She waved a hand towards the world outside. 'Nor would the entire Scottish nation.'

Isabel looked at the mozzarella on her plate. She thought of buffaloes. Then she thought of the entire Scottish nation, and how it might be watching the outcome of the Portrait Gallery advisory committee's power struggles with bated breath. She laughed.

'I overstate,' said Laura.

'You do. But why not?'

'Why not indeed?' said Laura, and then, as if to put the whole matter in perspective, she said, 'This carrot and coriander soup is delicious.'

It was a signal for a change of subject – a switch to the safer realm of soup and salad, topics which rarely involved rancour. But Isabel had a final remark to add.

'Lettuce is very ambitious,' she said.

'Yes, but I'm not going to be pushed around by a . . . Lettuce,' Laura said.

They both laughed. 'Good luck,' said Isabel. 'I'm not sure if I shall be able to do much to help you, though. I'm terribly busy at present.' She paused. 'Do you mind if I ask how you came to be on the committee? I'm not all that sure why I'm there, you see.'

Laura said that she understood why Isabel should ask that question. 'A lot of committees in this city have the same small gene pool in them,' she said. 'There are people who show willing and then their names are on the ... what do you call that thing that people used to have? The thing for names?'

'Rolodex,' said Isabel. 'I think they still exist, in spite of computers. The metaphor remains. And people like something tangible.'

'Well, I must have got onto the Great Rolodex – somehow. And then ... ' She hesitated, as if uncertain whether to confide in Isabel. 'Well, my husband has been generous in his donations. He's given quite a bit of support to the museum and to the galleries too.'

'I see,' said Isabel. 'That might be the case with me, as well. In fact, I suspect it is. That's one way onto the Rolodex.'

'Anyway, I'm interested in portraiture,' said Laura. 'I chose history of art as one of my courses at St Andrews back in the day. I started a thesis on Allan Ramsay but didn't get very far. I met Bruce and then ... ' She shrugged. 'Then came two children, followed by life in general.'

'I have two children,' said Isabel. 'I know what that means.'

'Mine are both grown-up now,' said Laura. 'But ... ' She looked away, and then turned to face Isabel again. 'Actually, I have something to confess. I was hoping to be able to talk to you about them. You see, I've heard ... '

She did not finish the sentence, but Isabel sensed what was coming. This was what Jamie had warned her about, time and time again. Word got out that you helped people, and then the requests came in – the thinly veiled pleas, the hints, the overt and unignorable cries for help. And this was exactly how they arose – incidentally, unexpectedly, when you thought you would be talking about something else.

'Please tell me,' Isabel said. 'I don't mind – I really don't.'

We repeat our mistakes, she thought. We know what they are, and we may even know why we make them, where we stumble, where we forget the lines we should be saying and instead say those things we know we should not say. And so we repeat ourselves, making the same error again and again, creating for ourselves familiar difficulties that we know we should avoid, but never do. And yet, and yet ... How could anyone say to another: I don't want to hear what you have to say? She could not, and she *would* not.

4

Jamie did the cooking that night. They had slipped into a routine, without ever having discussed it. That, thought Isabel, was the best sort of rota – one that came about through custom and long practice. An *organic* rota, one might call it. Unless he had a musical engagement, Jamie now cooked on Monday nights – 'because it's Monday, and I know how hard Mondays are,' he had said; on Wednesday nights – 'I've always cooked on Wednesdays, even as a boy'; on Friday nights – 'I love cooking on a Friday because the weekend is coming up and I feel ... well, I just feel like being in the kitchen, having a glass of wine at the chopping board ...'; and on Saturdays – 'Saturday is such a ... sorry, there's no other word for it, such a *sexy* night and cooking, as we all know, is sublimation ...' Which left Tuesday, Thursday, and, finally, Sunday, when Jamie did not like cooking because Sunday evening had always been difficult for him – a *dreich* evening, he said, using the Scots word for dreary and over-cast. 'That,' he said, 'must be the fault of our Presbyterian heritage in Scotland. It cast such a gloom over Sundays, while Mediterranean Catholicism always seemed to be full of noise and fun.' Isabel thought about that explanation; he was probably right, she decided: there was too much *conscience* in a Scottish Sunday.

But now it was Friday evening, and Jamie had been perusing his recipe books while Isabel settled the boys. She had read them two stories that night rather than one, because the first had been shorter than usual and this had led to a howl of protest. At no age is the human instinct for fairness more highly developed than in the years before seven, and both Charlie and Magnus had insisted that fairness required a second story to make up for the brevity of the first. Isabel had conceded, with the result that by the time she came down to the kitchen, Jamie had chosen and begun to make the first of the two courses he was planning to cook.

'I decided on a crab soufflé,' he said to her, as she accepted the glass of chilled white wine he had poured. 'We happened to have some crab.'

'Heaven,' she said: of the soufflé, of the wine, or of simply being in the kitchen together – it could have been any of these.

'And then a stuffed aubergine dish I found in my Julia Child.'

'She was without fault,' said Isabel.

The soufflé required his attention. The recipe came from a restaurant on a small Hebridean island, Scalpay, where the seafood was landed outside the kitchen window. The crab was Hebridean too, but from Mull, brought over by a friend of Jamie's who played the accordion in a traditional band and harvested seafood in his spare time.

'This couldn't be simpler,' said Jamie. 'You start with a roux and everything falls into place thereafter. The goat's cheese must be mild, though. It mustn't fight with the crab.'

'No,' said Isabel, not paying much attention. 'I had lunch today.'

Jamie looked up from his saucepan. 'You do have an appetite, I hope.'

Isabel reassured him. 'I had mozzarella and tomatoes. I've got plenty of room.'

'I could scrap the aubergines,' said Jamie. 'We could have the soufflé with salad.'

'No,' said Isabel. 'I love aubergines. But lunch ... I was going to have it by myself – reading. I spent the whole morning writing letters and I wanted a bit of time to unwind. But I met somebody – or rather she met me.'

Jamie began to add the goat's cheese to his roux. 'Oh yes. And?'

'A woman called Laura. She's married to a man called Bruce Douglas. She's the chair of—'

Jamie interrupted her. 'Bruce Douglas? I know that name. He's a big supporter of various orchestras – and of Scottish Opera too, I think. His name's always in the programmes – you know, in the lists of those who sponsor particular productions, that sort of thing.'

'That's him,' said Isabel. 'She said something about his support for the arts.'

'Somebody told me where the money comes from,' said Jamie. 'They were big wine importers from way back. They still do that, but I think they have other strings to their bow. Anyway, they're generous.'

'And unhappy,' said Isabel.

Jamie looked up. 'She said that?'

'Yes. She said the family's ... well, she said it's unhappy.'

Jamie shrugged. 'What's the line from Tolstoy? "All happy families are alike. Unhappy families are unhappy in their particular way."'

'*Anna Karenina*,' said Isabel. 'I've often thought about that line. I'm not sure it's true. People often don't appreciate how complex happiness may be. They think that happy people are shallow, which can be so wrong. It's actually far easier to be unhappy than it is to be happy. It requires more effort, more understanding, more character to be consistently happy.'

'Perhaps,' said Jamie. He looked onquiringly at Isabel. 'You're happy, aren't you?'

She did not hesitate. 'Of course I am.'

'And so am I,' said Jamie. 'Although sometimes I wake up at night and think that my happiness could end. Suddenly. Just like that. I think that something dreadful could happen and it would be over.'

'Those thoughts,' said Isabel, 'occur in the small hours because one's blood sugar is low. It's all to do with metabolism. Three o'clock in the morning is a melancholy time.'

'The hour of the wolf. That's what the Irish call it,' said Jamie. 'At least that's what an Irish friend told me. He had a good imagination, of course.' He paused. 'But why are they unhappy – these Douglases? Did she tell you?'

Isabel replied that Laura had confided in her. 'I was a bit surprised, but she didn't hold back. I hadn't met her before, but it all came out.'

Jamie began to whisk some egg whites. 'There are some people like that. You meet them on trains, in cafés – anywhere, really. They unburden themselves even if you barely know them. I don't know why they do it.'

Isabel knew. She was not surprised to hear that Jamie was confided in. People talked to him because they were attracted to beauty. It was a truth that the beautiful themselves often failed to grasp.

She took another sip of her wine. She would have to

tell him, and this was as good a time as any to do so. 'She wanted my help.'

Jamie increased the speed of his whisking. 'I see.'

She looked at him anxiously. 'I know what you feel about these things.'

He concentrated on the egg whites. He did not say anything.

'I could hardly say no. All she wanted me to do was to speak to her children.'

'Is that all?'

Isabel nodded. 'Yes. She asked me to act as a sort of go-between.'

'Hopeless,' muttered Jamie. 'If it's got that bad, then a go-between isn't going to make much difference.'

The soufflé mixture could be stored in the fridge, and he did that before attending to the aubergines. 'What's their problem?' he asked over his shoulder.

'They disagree,' said Isabel.

'What family doesn't?'

'Very few, I imagine,' said Isabel. 'But this one's badly split. It's political, apparently.'

Jamie had already salted the aubergines to remove the bitterness. Now he wiped away the beads of vegetable perspiration. 'There must be something more than that. People can vote in different ways from their parents or siblings or whatever and still not be at each other's throats.'

Isabel agreed with that. She and her niece, Cat, took a different view of politics. Cat often expressed admiration for the sort of conviction politician whom Isabel found unsympathetic, while she herself tended to admire those who were more liberal, more forgiving, in their views. They avoided political disagreement, though, by simply staying away from subjects where it might be expected to arise. She knew that nothing she said would disabuse Cat of her convictions, and Cat, she imagined, felt the same about her and her views. And that tolerance extended to friends, as well: and perhaps even went too far. Isabel had a friend who was an avowed communist, even to the extent of denying the manifest faults of the Soviet Union. 'They tried so hard,' this friend said, 'but the machinations of international capitalism were just too much for them to deal with. They almost made it – almost. It was such a tragedy.'

Isabel had listened to this, and other remarks of the sort, without saying much. At length she had simply said, 'And the Gulag? And Stalin's Terror?'

'Exaggerated,' said her friend.

'And the pact with Nazi Germany?'

The friend had shaken her head. 'That old canard! What choice did they have?'

'I think we should talk about something else,' said Isabel.

And her friend had quickly agreed, and the conversation had switched to poetry – her friend was a devotee of Edward Thomas – and they had discussed whether Thomas was a better poet than Robert Graves. They did not agree on that, but it did not matter, as no friendship would flounder on the rocks of poetic taste – or would it? thought Isabel.

But now Jamie was asking for more details. 'Did she give you any idea of what was behind it – apart from politics?'

'They have a son and a daughter,' said Isabel. 'Richard and Stephanie. She's older than her brother. She's twenty-six, I think Laura said. Richard's twenty-three. Stephanie's engaged to a man she met in London, and he's taking a job in Edinburgh to be near her. Richard graduated a year or two ago – in Scottish history. They don't talk to one another, this brother and sister. Stephanie speaks to her father, but not to her mother – or barely speaks to her. Richard won't speak to his sister or his father, but will speak to his mother.'

Jamie rolled his eyes. 'What did Tolstoy say?'

Isabel continued. 'The mother – Laura – thinks that her son is mostly at fault. She thinks that he's been turned against the family by some friend of his. She says this person – the friend – has an inordinate degree of influence over her son and is . . . well, she suggested he was actually brainwashing him.'

'Cult stuff?' asked Jamie.

'Not quite. I know that happens with cults—'

Jamie interrupted her. 'You don't have to be the follower of some zany guru to be turned against your family. There are plenty of apparently respectable religions that will do that for you.'

'Yes,' said Isabel. 'I know. In this case, she says the influence is more personal. This man – it's another young man, apparently – has enthused her son politically. The issue is where Scotland should be. That one.'

Jamie shrugged. 'Not a great surprise. Look at the facts. The population of Scotland is divided roughly down the middle on that. Gilbert and Sullivan could have written a song about it . . .' He paused. 'Or have they already done that? *Iolanthe*. Remember? *Every child that's born alive is either a little Liberal or else a little Conservative* . . . Same with this issue, don't you think?'

'Yes,' said Isabel. But she was not ready for levity just yet. 'I'd never say that believing in Scottish independence doesn't make any sense at all. It's an arguable option. Of course it is.'

'Norway, Sweden, Denmark – they seem to survive,' Jamie pointed out. 'They're small too.'

'Sweden's not all that small,' Isabel corrected him, and then asked, 'How many of us are there?'

Jamie had this sort of figure at his fingertips. It was a male thing, Isabel had always pointed out, with some amusement. Men read *Guinness World Records* when they were teenage boys and never seemed to forget the facts and figures it contained. They knew the height of Everest and the land-speed record and things of that ilk; women, she playfully suggested, had better things to think about. *Guinness World Records* was a book without characters and no discernible plot, she said; not one for the book club. But sometimes it was useful.

'There are slightly more Danes than Scots,' he said. '5.8 million of them and 5.4 million of us. Norway's not far behind us.'

'But those countries are very rich,' said Isabel. She wondered, though, whether being very rich gave you a greater right to self-determination. It seemed to, she thought. And that, surely, was wrong.

'The point that people make is this,' Jamie continued. 'If those Scandinavian countries can be independent states, then why can't Scotland?'

'Yes,' said Isabel. 'It's a perfectly coherent political position. Not everyone holds it – obviously. Reasonable people disagree on it. Obviously. We all have close friends who are in favour of leaving, and close friends who aren't.'

Jamie nodded. 'People should agree to differ.'

'But increasingly they don't.'

'No.' He looked thoughtful. 'Perhaps it's because it's difficult to contemplate being in two places at the same time – whatever the physicists may say.'

Isabel thought of her cousins in Dallas, Texas and Mobile, Alabama. One was a Democrat and another a Republican. They had stopped sending birthday cards to one another. 'I can't sit down at the same table with her,' Dallas had said of Mobile. 'Ever again. I just can't. Not until they enfranchise the residents of DC. To take just one example.'

'You could discuss that over dinner,' Isabel had suggested, only half seriously.

'No. Impossible.'

'You don't have a long enough spoon? Is that what you're saying?'

Now Jamie brought the conversation back to Scotland. 'It's trite, I know, but there are always two sides to these matters, aren't there?' Then he added, 'Not that you'd think that, listening to some people.'

'What Laura feels,' Isabel continued, 'is that her son has been persuaded to demonise anybody who disagrees with him. He says that he has accused his own father, her husband, of being a traitor to Scotland because he happens to support the constitutional status quo.'

Jamie shook his head. 'Scottish nationalists are not necessarily extremists — far from it. But some of them really do despise anybody who disagrees with them. They don't understand that people might want to be part of a bigger union. They don't want to share with others or co-operate. They're—'

'And there are those on the other side who can be equally intolerant,' Isabel pointed out. 'And that's the tragedy, I think. They're two groups of people who both want the same thing — the good of Scotland — but who have such very different ideas about how that might be achieved.'

Jamie sighed. 'I know. And we seem stuck in this perpetual shouting match with one another. Just like so many other countries.'

'What we all need to do is co-operate more,' said Isabel. 'We won't solve the world's problems by trying to look after ourselves and not paying any attention to the needs of others. That just won't work.' She paused. 'We have to love one another a bit more, I think.'

She thought of Auden and his famous, suppressed poem 'September 1, 1939' with its controversial line 'We must love one another or die'. Auden disliked the poem, which he came to view as insincere and simply wrong: we died whether or not we loved one another. Yet people liked that ending because it reflected what they felt about the need for love in human affairs. And people recognised, too, Isabel thought, the truth in those lines from the same poem: 'I and the public know/ What all schoolchildren learn,/Those to whom evil is done/ Do evil in return.'

Jamie was thinking of the more immediate problem of Richard Douglas. 'Does Richard's mother expect you to get him out of the hands of this Svengali? To mount a rescue mission?'

'She wants me to talk to him,' said Isabel. 'That's all.'

'I don't see what good that will do. Does she think you'll be able to persuade him that his whole political outlook is wrong? People don't change just like that – not on a fundamental matter of belief.'

'No,' said Isabel. 'But I might be able to tell him that it's not helpful to describe his own father as a traitor.'

Jamie looked doubtful. 'Bigotry isn't that easy to dismantle, you know. People with immoveable views dig in, which is why their views are immoveable.'

Isabel threw a glance at the fridge. 'Are we going to eat that soufflé?' she asked. 'Or just imagine it?'

Jamie laughed. 'I'll get the ramekins.'

Isabel took another sip of her wine. Two glasses, she said to herself: one to unwind, and one to make the world seem a nicer place than it actually was – to make one think that antagonistic divisions might in due course be replaced by courtesy and understanding of the other's viewpoint. Things that once had been there, but seemed to have been forgotten in the shrill exchanges of our times. You could hope; more than that, you *had* to hope. Or you cried, perhaps, or felt the urge to cry, and held back the tears somehow, but not always ...

'Isabel?'

Jamie was staring at her. He had picked up a tea towel that he had been using to wipe a plate. The tea towel bore a picture of Robert Burns, a mouse, and a sheaf of wheat. There were thousands of these tea towels out there in the world – the necessary indignity visited upon a national poet. Grace had given it to Isabel on her last birthday, along with a tinned Dundee cake and a bunch of flowers from the florist at Church Hill.

'Isabel? What's wrong?'

He handed her the tea towel, for her tears.

She shook her head. 'Nothing.' She wiped her cheeks. 'Nothing's wrong. I don't know. Sorry.'

He came to her side and bent down to put his arms about her. He did this with such tenderness, she noticed. 'Why are you crying?'

She leaned against him. She saw a trace of flour on his hands, from the making of the soufflé. She tried to explain, although she sensed that he understood and that no explanation was really necessary. There were things that were difficult to put into words, and that, of course, was why there were tears. Tears were more eloquent, made the point more forcefully, and, unlike words, could be faked only with difficulty, and with a skill that few of us possessed. Tears meant what they failed to say.

'Is it to do with what we were talking about? About people being at one another's throats?'

She nodded. That was one way of putting it – and probably the best one. 'I just wish,' she said, 'that we had peace. Does that make sense to you?'

'Of course it does. Of course. It's what we all want, I think.'

He kissed her lightly on the cheek. It was the sort of kiss they gave the boys – to make it better. A child fell, and we kissed things better, and miraculously the pain of the fall disappeared. Perhaps that might continue into adulthood, as now, so that a kiss might relieve the pain.

'I hate politics,' said Jamie, standing up again. 'I'm glad I'm a musician, and not a politician.'

'And yet politics are inevitable, don't you think?'

Jamie grinned. 'As is music – thankfully.'

'What we hate is the wrong sort of politics.'

He thought about that. She was right. But he was surprised by her crying.

'Are you feeling better?' he asked.

'Yes, I am. Although I feel a bit foolish, crying like that. I suppose it's just that it all suddenly seemed too much.'

He returned to the soufflé, which he now put in the oven. 'This will be done in no time. I'll lay the table.'

'No, let me. Please let me.'

She found the cutlery and the table napkins. And the salt and pepper, both of which needed filling.

'We really should eat less salt,' she said, as she poured the flakes into the grinder. 'Pure, the gift of the seas', the box proclaimed.

'Oh, I know,' said Jamie. 'We should do less of everything.'

'Well, not *everything*.'

They laughed.

'Be careful,' he said suddenly, dropping his voice. 'Getting involved with those people. I know I can't stop you. I know it's what you do – or what you feel you have to do. I know that. But please be careful.'

She thought about his words. *What you feel you have to do . . .*

Yes, he was right: she did feel that she had to do this sort of thing. It was not because she was weak-willed and could not say no. She had to do what she did because she was in a position to do it. She was well off. She had help in the house. She had time. These things had just come to her, it seemed, as her lot in life, but she could not take them for granted; she could not conduct herself as if they were somehow her due. She had to give something back – to be useful. Did that make sense, or did it sound pious? Did she even have to think about it?

'I shall.'

He served the soufflé.

'This is just so delicious,' Isabel said.

He looked at her over the top of his wine glass and smiled. 'I love you so much,' he said.

The telephone rang.

'Let's not answer,' said Jamie, adding with a smile, 'What's there to say, anyway?'

5

The telephone call had been from Cat, and it had ruined the evening for Isabel – and, she suspected, for Jamie, although he had the stuffed aubergines to keep him busy.

'Are you around tomorrow?' Cat had asked. 'Mid-morning?'

It had taken Isabel a few moments to regain her composure. She had not seen Cat for more than six months, and had believed her to be in . . . She thought quickly: the Windward Islands, or was it the Leeward? But then it came back to her, and she remembered *Antigua, Penny, Puce*, the title of a novel by Robert Graves that had stuck in her mind years earlier and had stayed there, as a line of poetry, or of song, can do. 'Antigua, Penny, Puce' was a stamp . . . the unintended poetry of philately.

'Aren't you in Antigua?' was all she could think of to say. There had been an email, with an accompanying photograph, taken on board a yacht, with a tiny, red-roofed church in the background. 'You sound as if you're in—'

'In Morningside,' interjected Cat. 'Which is exactly where

I am. Balcarres Street. Remember my friend, Helen? The one who won that cookery competition − although her cooking, frankly, is rubbish. Her. I'm staying with her.'

'I see.' Isabel did not remember Helen. But how, she thought, could you stay with somebody and yet describe their cooking as rubbish − while under their roof? That was the problem with Cat, thought Isabel: there was a moral casualness about her. If you accepted somebody's hospitality, you did not describe their cooking as rubbish, or at least you did not do so *needlessly*.

'I meant to tell you I'd be in Edinburgh,' Cat continued, 'but things have been happening and you know how it is.'

There was a silence, and Isabel realised that Cat expected Isabel to confirm that she did, in fact, know how things were.

'Yes, of course. Busy. Same as ever.'

'You can say that again,' Cat agreed. 'There's a lot to discuss. We won't know where to start.'

'Of course. Antigua, and ... and so much more.' Isabel paused. 'Is Leo with you?'

There was another silence. Dead, Isabel thought suddenly. Leo would be dead. People like Leo did things that ... that made them dead.

Finally, 'Leo's in Belize,' Cat replied. There was no further explanation.

A dangerous place, thought Isabel. Even if you weren't dead when you first went to Belize, there was always a possibility that you soon would be.

'Belize?' said Isabel.

'Yes. He took the boat. You know the boat we bought in Oban? The one we said we'd sail down to the Azores? We made the crossing to Antigua.'

'Yes.'

'Well, he's taken it to Belize now. He's going to charter it out there once the hurricane season's over. He's already got some bookings. There are some people from England and a French group. He's going to be busy.'

Isabel hesitated. 'You aren't going to crew for him, then?'

Cat did not reply immediately. Through the phone line, Isabel imagined she felt a bristling resentment.

'Leo and I have agreed to go our separate ways,' Cat said at last. 'Amicably. No hard feelings.'

Isabel drew in her breath. The marriage had lasted slightly less than a year. That had been typical of Cat's relationships in the past, but she had thought that perhaps it would be different with marriage. She had actually married Leo, and Isabel had imagined that this might mean a greater degree of perman- ence. But obviously she'd been wrong. Why bother to get married when your record was one of impermanence?

'We're both enjoying being single,' Cat went on. 'Leo has a new girlfriend – I must tell you about her. A big-time airhead, but if that's what he wants, that's what he wants. And I'm with somebody new too.'

Isabel closed her eyes. Nothing had changed.

'I look forward to meeting him,' she said. 'Perhaps the two of you could come round for supper – something like that.'

'Possibly. But look, I must go. Can you meet me for coffee tomorrow morning?'

'Of course,' replied Isabel. 'At the deli? I'm sure Eddie would like to see you.'

'Dear Eddie,' said Cat. 'He's so sweet.'

'I'm not sure he'd like to be described as sweet,' said Isabel. 'Few young men do – even when they are.'

'They shouldn't try too hard,' said Cat, rather enigmatically. 'But no, let's meet in that French bakery place. What's it called? "La" something . . .'

'La Barantine.'

They made the arrangement, and Isabel put down the receiver. She looked at Jamie, who made a face. 'I only heard one side of that conversation,' he said. 'But I assume that Leo's history.'

'Ancient history,' said Isabel. 'Pre-Roman.'

'I could have warned him,' said Jamie.

'Or her,' said Isabel. 'Don't assume it's her fault.'

'You're right,' said Jamie. 'I know we're all meant to assume that break-ups are not anybody's fault, but that's so obviously false. You can't destroy the notion of fault in human relationships just by saying it doesn't exist.'

Isabel smiled. 'Can't you? Isn't that just what we're asked to do? To pretend that things are not what they so patently are?'

Jamie sighed. 'I wish we were back in the age of reason,' he said. 'Where are Voltaire, Rousseau, Hume?'

'Where indeed?' asked Isabel.

'Instead of which, we find ourselves in a climate of unthinking conformity. Nobody thinks any longer.'

'That's a bit extreme,' said Isabel. 'Most people think; it's just that they don't think, well, all the time.'

They both laughed at that, although Isabel found herself thinking of what Jamie had said and of how high the stakes were. Unthinking conformity; a failure to question ... We assumed that we would always have benevolent government; we assumed that our democracies would survive, that there would be no recurrence of the horrors and darkness that had taken place barely more than a generation before our own – the Holocaust, brutal fascism, the terrors of Stalin, Mao, Pol Pot – but keeping such atavism at bay depended on *thinking*, on the defence of truth and reason, on defending freedom and the values attached to it. These were barricades that still needed to be manned, because there were still those prepared to shout those values down, still those prepared to say that truth does not exist and that right and wrong are arbitrary preferences, no more than that.

Then Isabel looked serious again. 'Oh, I wish Cat would ...' She was not sure how to finish.

'... would change?' suggested Jamie. 'But people don't, do they?'

Isabel had to agree that they did not. Cat had not changed at all as far as she could make out. If anything, she had grown worse. That was change of a sort, Isabel reflected. And if you could get worse, then presumably, by the same token, you could get better. Perhaps getting rid of Leo represented the beginning of an improvement. But that would depend on what this new, currently unnamed man was like. She was not hopeful.

La Barantine, a small French bakery, served coffee and light lunches. Isabel bought croissants and baguettes there several mornings a week, and met friends there too over a cup of café au lait; she had expected Cat to suggest that they should meet in what Isabel still called Cat's deli, even if it now belonged to Isabel, through a trust. Was there an issue there? she wondered. Cat had willingly sold her interest in the deli, but Isabel reminded herself that people sometimes resented even those things they did voluntarily.

Cat was late, and Isabel was beginning to wonder whether she had got the time wrong when her niece eventually arrived.

'I'm sorry if you've been waiting for ages,' Cat said, unwinding a light silk scarf she was wearing. 'I was stopped four times walking up Morningside Road — *four* times! People who used to be customers of the deli. And of course, they wanted to catch up.'

Isabel reassured her that she did not mind. 'Don't worry. I had things to think of.'

Cat's eyes widened. 'Oh really? Such as?'

Isabel felt slightly irritated: she felt you should not ask others what they were thinking of – it seemed intrusive because those of whom it was asked might be thinking of something private, and would then be forced to lie.

'Nothing much,' she replied. That was, strictly speaking, true.

Cat sat down. 'They all asked me when I would be going back to the deli,' she said. 'It's good to be missed.'

Isabel said nothing.

'They said they hoped I'd be back,' Cat persisted.

Isabel swallowed hard. She had not anticipated that Cat would return and try to unpick the arrangements that had been made. This was far from welcome news.

'Eddie seems to be coping fine,' said Isabel. 'And Hannah too.'

Hannah was the manager who had been appointed to run the deli after Cat's departure. She had proved to be a good choice as she seemed to get on well with everybody – with their suppliers as well as with Eddie and the customers. If Cat was implying that the customers were not content with the new management, then this would be the first that Isabel had heard of it.

'I told them, of course, that I wouldn't be returning,' Cat continued.

Isabel relaxed.

'The trouble with some people,' Cat continued, 'is that they want things to remain the same – or even to go back to the way they were before. And that's just not possible.'

'No,' said Isabel, not without relief. 'It just isn't. And fortunately, there's no need for that with the deli . . . ' She stopped.

She was aware that Cat had fixed her with an intense gaze. Hurriedly, she corrected herself. 'I don't mean that things didn't work well in the past. I didn't mean that.'

'No?'

'No. Definitely not. It's just that everything seems to be going rather well. Eddie's working hard but doesn't have to worry about the bigger picture. Hannah does all that.'

Cat did not seem to be interested. 'They're welcome to it,' she said airily. 'All that messy cheese.' She wrinkled her nose. 'Having to wipe surfaces all the time. Having to wash your hands fifteen times a day. All that smelly stuff.'

But cheese is always smelly, thought Isabel. *Life* itself is a smelly business. And you can't wave smells away just like that.

She did not let her disagreement show. Cat liked an argument, and there was no point in rubbing her up the wrong way. And Cat, in spite of everything, was family. 'I see. Well, you don't need to, do you? You can afford to wait for the right job to crop up – that is, if you're thinking of working.'

'Of course I'm going to work,' snapped Cat. 'Not everyone can—' She stopped herself, but Isabel knew what she'd been going to say. She would have gone on to refer to those who had money and did not have to worry about having a job. That was unfair; Isabel had always worked, and always would. She did not believe in living off unearned income. Her job – editing the *Review* – was demanding, as was the *Review* itself. She paid for that. She paid the printing bills; hers, unlike most academic journals, made generous payments to the contributors, book reviewers, and members of the editorial board. Others shamelessly exploited such people – often even requiring those who wrote for their journals to pay large sums for the honour of publication. The owners knew that people would accede to such preposterous requests because they were so desperate to be published. This meant that predatory journals flourished – prepared to accept anything, as long as the authors made the payments they demanded. Inevitably, these journals were unmasked from time to time when they accepted for publication deliberately contrived nonsense. These exposés had included cases in which articles on subjects such as nuclear physics had been written by those with no knowledge of the subject, and had been readily accepted by unscrupulous editors.

'Isabel?'

'Sorry, I was thinking of something else.'

Cat gave a thin smile. 'You always are. I was telling you about my plan. You were miles away.'

Isabel made an apologetic gesture. 'You have my full attention. I promise.'

'Gordon and I are planning to open a shop.'

Isabel wanted to know about Gordon first; the shop could wait. 'Tell me about Gordon.' And then she added, 'I'm sorry about Leo.'

That was not true. She was not sorry about Leo, and she thought that Cat would probably sense that. But Cat simply nodded and said, 'Thanks. Leo and I were on different vectors.'

Isabel stared at her.

'Don't look so surprised,' said Cat, rather testily. 'Some people *are* just on different vectors. It happens.'

Isabel nodded. She was struggling with the role of vectors in relationships. Were Jack Sprat and his wife simply on different vectors?

'And he couldn't resist younger women,' Cat went on. 'He couldn't help himself.'

'I see,' said Isabel.

'Not that I blame him. Not entirely.'

'No?'

'No. Men feel these things. I think sometimes we women don't understand just how powerful male urges can be.'

Isabel was not sure what to say. Everyone has urges, she thought, except for those lucky few who ... who have no urges. But you could not let your urges determine what you did. Controlling our urges was what set us aside as a species. It was what lay at the heart of human civilisation, the whole edifice of which was based on the notion that urges were held in check. Principalities, cathedrals, museums, great works of art – all of these came into existence because urges were sublimated. Even books on sublimation required sublimation.

She met Cat's gaze. 'I don't think urges are always an excuse,' she said.

It was a mildly voiced objection, but Cat was defensive. 'I didn't say they were. All I'm saying is that you have to understand. You can't blame men if every so often they give in.'

'To these urges they have?'

'Yes.'

Isabel stared at Cat. She wondered whether she was being ironic. Her grandmother might have said such a thing, or one of her aunts in Mobile – to hear it from Cat, though, seemed anachronistic. 'You mean that men are weak? Is that what you're saying?'

Cat nodded. 'They're weak.'

Yes, thought Isabel, she means it, even if she sounded like one of Barbara Pym's spinsters pronouncing on the needs of men.

Seemingly unaware of the effect of her words, Cat continued, 'Leo was strong – to look at, but underneath he was weak.'

Isabel smiled. 'Yes, he did look strong. I thought he looked just like a lion.'

This was not well received. 'Like a lion? Just because of his name?'

Isabel's tone was placatory. 'Not because of his name. His arms.' They had been muscular, and covered with fine yellow hair. 'And his hair. That mane of . . . '

She did not finish; judging by Cat's expression, a line had apparently been crossed. 'What was wrong with his hair? You can't judge people by their hair, you know.'

Isabel sought to redirect the conversation. 'He went off to Belize, you said. Is he happy there?'

'He's doing fine,' said Cat. 'He has this American girlfriend with him, on the boat. She's called Polly. She's twenty – just. Not known for her intellect. Her head's full of chewing gum, I think. But he seems to like her.'

'Oh well.' It must be something to do with urges, thought Isabel.

'I've forgiven Leo,' Cat said.

'Good. That's what we have to do. We have to forgive.' Isabel paused. 'And Gordon? Where did you meet?'

Cat replied that it had been in Antigua. 'We were in Jolly Harbour – you may have heard of it. It's a big sailing place. And he was cooking on a boat owned by a Canadian. Some guy who owns a timber company, a big one. Anyway, it was a fancy boat and Gordon was covering for the chef they'd lost. He fell overboard, apparently. They went back to look for him, but they never found him. Gordon was the yacht's sous chef, you see, and so they promoted him.'

'Most unfortunate,' said Isabel. 'Losing a chef like that.'

Cat agreed. 'Very. Gordon never liked him much, though. He said he was greedy.'

'I suspect many chefs are,' said Isabel. 'I suppose they feel an urge to eat.'

Cat gave her a sideways glance. 'And if he didn't like one of the guests,' she went on, 'he would spit in that person's soup. Gordon asked him not to, and he just laughed. He said, "Chef's privilege – and they deserve it."'

There was more to the story. 'Gordon would never spit in anybody's soup. Never. And he felt he couldn't sit back and let this happen. He felt sorry for the guests, because the chef always ended up not liking one or two of them, and then he would start his spitting campaigns.'

Isabel winced. She remembered the expression 'worse things happen at sea'. Well, this was one of those things, she decided.

'Gordon has a really strong sense of right and wrong,' Cat said. 'He thought it was wrong to spit in somebody's soup.'

Undoubtedly, thought Isabel. She found it difficult to think of any moral philosophers who would not have condemned it out of hand. 'Was he able to do anything about it?'

'He went to the captain and told him.'

'That was probably the right thing to do,' said Isabel. And yet she was familiar with the issues around whistle-blowing: the sound of the whistle was often picked up by the miscreant even before the authorities noticed it. And the authorities, of course, might be deaf to the warning, while the miscreants themselves rarely were. She thought for a moment, inconsequentially, of how a whistle-blower's personal crest might look – the sort of device that families in the ascendant used to make for themselves, complete with motto. *I sound the alarm* might be a suitable motto for such a person: *clangorem clamo*, and the device itself might be a trumpet, or perhaps even a goose – because it was the geese, was it not, that had saved Rome?

'A Capitoline goose,' she muttered. 'The geese at Juno's temple heard the Gauls . . . ' She stopped. There was no point in talking to Cat about the Gauls.

69

Cat looked at her. 'What was that? Did you say something about geese?'

It was too complicated to explain, and Isabel urged Cat to continue. 'Pay no attention to me,' she said.

Cat resumed her story. 'The captain was livid. Gordon said he heard him shouting at the chef. He accused him of spitting in his own soup, but the chef said he would never do that. The captain said he didn't believe him. He called Gordon up to the bridge and asked him outright whether he had ever seen the chef spit in his soup. Gordon was really worried. He'd assumed his complaint was confidential. Now the chef knew – and he was famous for his bad temper.'

Isabel shook her head. 'It's difficult for whistle-blowers. People shouldn't reveal their identity like that.'

'No, they shouldn't,' agreed Cat. 'As they left the bridge, the chef said to Gordon that he would settle things with him. He said, "You're toast."'

'A serious threat in kitchen circles,' said Isabel.

'Gordon went back to the captain afterwards and told him that the chef had threatened him. The captain told him that he should lock himself in his cabin until they reached harbour. They were going to St Vincent. The captain said he would deal with the chef.' Cat paused. She looked thoughtful. 'That night the chef fell overboard.'

Isabel's eyes widened.

'That was the end of that,' said Cat. 'They found out later that the chef was wanted for murder in Martinique. Gordon stayed on board for another couple of months. Then he and I decided to come back to Scotland. He's from Paisley, you see. He's a really nice man, and we're going to open a coffee bar together. Not an ordinary coffee bar – we're going to sell single estate coffees, that sort of thing.'

'Where?' asked Isabel.

'Right here. Two doors down, in fact. I've got the lease.'

Isabel digested this information.

'And we'll sell some olives and olive oil. Gordon wants to bake. Croissants and baguettes will be up there – our main item, I think. We definitely don't want to do cheese, but we'll probably do some wine. Italian, I think, What's that stuff? Drunello. And some of those massive wines from Sicily. You know them? It's the volcanic soil down there – Etna and so on.' She smiled, as if recalling a fond memory. 'Gordon loves Italy. He can sing in Italian, you know. He worked there once, as a chef. In Ravenna. He cooked for a very rich Swede who lived in one of those massive farmhouses they have – it was more of a castle, Gordon said. The Swede was always giving parties. He was really small, this Swedish guy – Gordon said he was really some sort of dwarf. But he had lots of tall friends, and they had famous guests all the time. You should hear about some of the people Gordon's met. You wouldn't believe it.'

Cat named names, pausing after each, as if to allow its significance time to sink in. But few meant anything to Isabel. There was a tattooed footballer – she had never seen the point of him; there was a man who drove Formula One racing cars at over 200 miles per hour. *Why was he in such a hurry?* There was a woman who was famous for reasons nobody understood, but who became more famous each time she said something of surpassing fatuousness. Isabel could not remember what most of these people were called, but one name did resonate with her – that of a woman whose marriage had been all over the tabloid papers.

'*Her?*' said Isabel. 'He met her?'

Cat nodded. 'Yes, she came for a party and stayed all

71

weekend. Gordon said she brought sixteen suitcases. Sixteen – for two nights in the house.'

Isabel smiled. 'Some of these people have a lot of baggage.'

It took Cat a moment or two to react, but eventually she smiled back. 'Yes, you could say that. Louis Vuitton cases – you know the sort of thing.'

'No,' said Isabel. She was determined not to know anything about Louis Vuitton luggage because that was exactly what they wanted you to do – the manufacturers of these designer goods wanted people to know their brand name. That was what they set out to do: to worm their way into your consciousness. 'I don't recall ever having seen a Louis Vuitton suitcase.'

Cat looked incredulous. 'You must have seen them – if you've ever been to an airport.'

Isabel was determined not to concede. 'I'm not all that interested in other people's baggage,' she said. 'A suitcase is just a suitcase, after all. It's a functional object.'

'One of those cabin bags can cost almost two thousand pounds,' said Cat.

Isabel made a dismissive gesture. 'That proves my point,' she said. 'No cabin bag can possibly be worth two thousand pounds. Think what you could do with two thousand pounds in Malawi.'

Cat frowned. 'Why Malawi?'

'Because Malawi needs the money,' said Isabel. 'Two thousand pounds could start a workshop there. A business. They're nice people, the Malawians.'

Cat looked disgruntled. 'I don't see why you're going on about this. You can't judge people by their luggage.'

'But isn't that precisely what designer luggage invites us to do?'

'I don't see that.'

Isabel took a sip of her coffee. 'Let's not argue about Louis Vuitton bags. I'm sure they're very well made. Sturdy, even. And very smart – not that one needs sixteen of them for one weekend. Mind you ... ' She had remembered something. 'Have you heard of King Zog?'

Cat looked blank, and Isabel had to remind herself that Cat really knew very little about history: she'd once had to correct her when she had clearly confused the French and Russian revolutions. Isabel had been tactful, of course, and had reassured Cat: 'It's a very easy mistake to make – very easy.'

Now, she explained about King Zog. 'He was the King of Albania. That is, when Albania had a king. Zog more or less proclaimed himself. He eventually had to go into exile, and ended up living in England somewhere.' There was a drifting population of displaced royalty, she reminded herself; grand riff-raff, in so many cases – people who expected to be maintained at the expense of others, or who lived on what they had managed to get away with before their exile: jewels, paintings, such bawbees as they'd been able to salvage from their vanishing treasuries.

Cat looked uninterested.

'The reason I mention him,' Isobel continued, 'is that King Zog had over 2,000 suitcases with him when he went into exile. There were questions asked about it in the House of Commons.' She looked at Cat. 'He didn't travel light. Of course, he was coming for more than the weekend ... '

She put King Zog out of her mind and thought about the coffee shop. It sounded to her rather like a deli. 'Won't you be competition for Hannah and Eddie? They sell those things too. And coffee.'

Cat's manner was insouciant. 'They'll be a few doors away and competition is a good thing, anyway.'

'Possibly, but it's sure to take a certain amount of business away from them.'

Cat shrugged again. Then she said, 'I'd like you to meet Gordon.'

'Thank you.'

'He wants to meet you. He said he likes talking to older women.'

Isabel looked up at the sky through the window of La Barantine. This was typical of Cat: she simply did not think of the effect of her words. But she was not going to change and there was no point in taking offence. So Isabel simply remarked, 'I look forward to talking to him,' while she thought, as she struggled to control her resentment, I'm not *that* old: I have two very young sons. How could I be *that* old?

'Of course, I wouldn't call you old,' Cat said, as an after-thought. 'Just yet.'

'You're very kind,' said Isabel.

6

On the same day as her meeting with Cat, Isabel went to see Laura Douglas in her house off Colinton Road. This was just around the corner from her own house, no more than five minutes away, and Isabel reflected on how she must have walked past it on numerous occasions without really noticing it. Not that there was much to set it aside from any number of houses in the area, where two-storey stone villas, solid in all their Victorian confidence, looked out from behind well-kept gardens. Isabel's house also fell into this category, although her garden was larger than most in the vicinity, and for this reason had been singled out by Brother Fox as his particular territory. It may not have been of Serengeti dimensions, but it was large enough to provide him with the shelter he needed to shield from prying eyes the russet mysteries of his life. The Douglas garden was less private than Isabel's, and any passer-by who was interested might catch a glimpse of the small gazebo on one side of the house, and hear, too, the sound of water playing in the small fountain on the other. In the short driveway that led off the road, a large electric car was parked, linked by a thick cable to a hidden charging point. The whole feel of the house was one of quiet comfort and low-key prosperity. It was not showy or attention-seeking, and even the fantoosh car seemed modest enough, proclaiming, discreetly but unambiguously, the cautious values of the household.

Isabel pressed the bell marked 'Please Pull'. She smiled at the 'Please' – a human touch that was being edged out of such instructions. Buttons now simply said 'Press', which was more in keeping with the straightforward tone of life today. Signs said 'Walk' or 'Don't Walk'; they never said 'Please Don't Walk', which of course had a ring of despair about it: *we've told you so many times before not to walk* . . . And then Isabel realised that she had missed something. She re-examined the button she had just pressed. She had pressed it in spite of the clear instruction to pull. But you could not pull a button.

The door opened, and Laura Douglas stood before Isabel. She looked puzzled as she saw Isabel peering at the button and its sign.

'Is there something . . . '

Isabel looked up. 'Oh, I'm sorry . . . yes, I've just noticed that this little brass plaque says "Please Pull". I don't like to be pedantic, but shouldn't it read "Please Press"?'

Laura stepped out to join Isabel in her scrutiny of the sign. 'Well!' she exclaimed. 'That's indeed so. It does say "Please Pull". And you, quite rightly, pressed, rather than attempted to pull.'

'I suspect most people would have done the same,' said Isabel. 'It's obviously a button rather than one of those old bell-pulls – you know, the brass ones connected to a long wire with a bell suspended at the other end, somewhere at the back of the house.'

Laura nodded. 'Yes. And I think I know what's happened. When we first came here, nothing had been done to the house for decades. The person we bought it from was very . . .' She hesitated.

'Old?' prompted Isabel. It was a word that contemporary squeamishness was on the point of retiring, in favour of a euphemism. But what was wrong with *old*? It was ridiculous to elbow it out of the language in the same way as we were losing the verb *to die*. We all died, and no amount of suggesting that we passed could protect us from that fact. So, too, did we become old rather than becoming *senior* or *elderly* or even *fully mature*, like cheeses.

Laura appeared relieved that she could speak directly. 'Yes, very old. I believe she was close to one hundred.' She paused. 'And proud of it.'

'So she should be,' said Isabel. 'When I get to that stage – *if* I get there – I don't want anybody telling me I can't be *old*. I shall be happy to be described as *ancient*.' She thought for a moment. 'And then when I proceed to *die*, I shall be most annoyed if anybody says that I am simply *passing*. Passing *where*, might one ask? Not everyone believes that we go somewhere when we shrug off this mortal coil.'

Laura laughed. 'There's an expression for you.'

'Shrugging off this mortal coil?' said Isabel. 'Yes, it's a wonderful expression. It suggests a certain relief, doesn't it? It suggests that one might actually be rather relieved to get away from everything. *With one shrug we are free* . . . And then one might be described as *defunct*, which is a splendid way of putting it, isn't it? There's no arguing with being defunct – that's it, so to speak.'

'She spent her whole life in this house. She was born in what is now the dining room.'

'How very middle class,' mused Isabel. 'To be born in a *dining room*. Rather like being found in a handbag.'

'A handbag?' said Laura.

'A whole life in one place,' Isabel went on. 'An awful thought for some, but I'm not so sure.'

'It would have its consolations,' said Laura. 'As far as I'm concerned, I want to stay here for the rest of my life.'

'And the bell?'

'Of course – the bell. That sign was there when we still had a pull arrangement. We replaced it with a button.'

'That explains it,' said Isabel. 'A disparity.'

'Modern signs are all so plastic,' said Laura. 'We liked the brass, and decided to keep it.'

'Which was undoubtedly the right thing to do,' said Isabel. 'Aesthetically, that is, if not semiotically.'

Laura laughed. 'I can't believe we're having this conversation.'

'But we need to talk about these matters,' said Isabel. 'Things of no apparent importance are often things of great importance.'

Laura gestured for Isabel to follow her. 'You must come in. It's very rude of me to keep you there.'

Isabel followed her into the hall. There were flowers on the table, and their powerful scent reached her quickly. 'From your garden?'

Laura nodded. 'I spend a lot of time on it.'

Isabel thought of Voltaire. He said one had a duty to cultivate one's garden. *Il faut cultiver notre jardin.* But did he do that himself? Did Voltaire have a garden, and if so, did he cultivate it? Somehow she could not see Voltaire plucking out weeds or pruning roses. He presumably meant that one should get somebody to cultivate one's garden, it being implicit that enlightenment philosophers were not expected to get their hands too dirty.

Laura had said something to her, and she'd missed it, thinking of Voltaire and his garden. Of course he didn't really mean an actual garden; it was all metaphorical – as Voltaire himself eventually came to be. And metaphorical gardens were really very easy to look after, as long as they remained metaphorical.

Laura was looking at her expectantly.

'I'm sorry,' said Isabel. 'Those lovely flowers of yours made me think of something.'

'I said that my husband was looking forward to meeting you. Shall we go and join him?'

A door led off the hall into the drawing room. She saw the paintings first: the Fergusson naked woman, all flesh and angles; the Peploe view of Mull from Iona or Iona from Mull; the Blackadder with its prowling cats and convenient flowers. Then she saw the man getting up from his chair, laying aside a newspaper – that day's *Scotsman* – and coming forward to meet her.

They shook hands.

'I'm Bruce,' he said. 'And I take it you're Isabel Dalhousie.'

'Isabel and I have been talking about language and euphemism,' said Laura.

Bruce glanced at his wife, as if uncertain whether to take the remark seriously. Then he smiled. 'It's best to get things out of the way.'

Laura said, 'I shall make tea.' She turned to Isabel. 'Unless you'd like coffee?'

Isabel said that tea would suit her perfectly. She was looking at the Peploe, but looked away quickly. She remembered something her mother had told her. 'Never stare at other people's pictures,' she had said. 'It's bad manners.' She had never worked out why. Was it because you might be thought to be appraising their worth? 'Or look at the titles of the books on their shelves,' her mother had added. 'Definitely not that. Unless you do it discreetly. You can do anything, Isabel, as long as you do it discreetly.' But then her mother had paused, and said, 'Do I really mean that? No, perhaps not.'

'China? India?' Laura asked.

'Oh, India please,' said Isabel. People sometimes said 'builders' in answer to that question, but that implied that builders could not be expected to have sophisticated taste in tea. And that was condescending, because there was no reason why builders should not like China tea, or Earl Grey, for that matter. And perhaps some did.

Isabel glanced at Bruce. You might not be able to look at paintings or bookshelves, but you could certainly look at people.

He was a man in his late fifties, or thereabouts; tall, and on the thin side. He had what was called a Roman nose, although Isabel had always doubted that the Romans actually had such noses, which may have been accentuated by sculptors. Ancient busts were presumably not always the best of likenesses, either being works of flattery, or of the imagination. We really have no idea what Homer looked like, in spite of the marble busts in which he is represented with rather crude features. 'Not the sort of man you'd expect to write an awfully long poem,' Jamie had once remarked.

She saw, too, that Bruce had kind eyes; light blue, gentle. He was exactly as she'd imagined he might be – this owner of a stone Victorian villa, with its well-tended garden, a scion of a claret-importing family, the husband of a woman who was on a lot of committees, a reader of a cautious, middle-of-the-road newspaper like the *Scotsman*. There was nothing unsettling about him, and she warmed to him. This family schism would not be his fault ... She stopped herself. Appearances were deceptive. Every piece has a villain, and it could just as well be this man, for all his reassuring looks and unthreatening demeanour.

While Laura was out of the room, he asked Isabel about the Portrait Gallery committee. 'I'm not one for committees myself,' he said. 'But Laura's good at them. It's a talent, I think – being able to sit there and listen to other people going on and on.'

Isabel explained that she had yet to attend a meeting of this particular committee. She was about to say something about the gallery, but Bruce spoke instead. He said, 'She told me that she'd asked you to help us.'

He looked at her. This was entreaty.

She made a gesture of powerlessness. 'I'm not sure how much use I'll be.'

'It's worth trying,' he said. 'And we'd be so grateful.' He paused, and now he looked away. There was a movement on a branch of a shrub outside the window. A small bird. He was watching it.

'Our son, Richard,' he went on, 'has been taken away from us. Taken – and I mean taken. He has been poisoned against us by another young man who has ...' He swallowed. She noticed the pain, which was of a particular and recognisable sort – that which is triggered in a parent by a child's misfortune. He struggled to finish. 'Poisoned by another young man who has some sort of power over him.'

He turned back to Isabel. 'I know that sounds melodramatic.'

She shook her head. 'No. I wouldn't say that.'

Laura had entered the room silently. She lowered the tray she was carrying, and placed it on a table. She began to pour tea into a cup. 'He's called Paul,' she said. 'The other boy, that is.'

'Men,' Bruce corrected her. 'They're not boys any longer.'

'Oh, I know, I know. It's just when it's your own son you still think of him as being a boy. I can't help it, really. He's still ... my little boy.'

A warning bell sounded. This was exactly what could drive a wedge between mother and son, thought Isabel. Mothers who found it hard to let go often drove their sons away. And as she thought about this, Isabel was again reminded of the futility of her involvement in this family's affairs. Family pathology was usually deep-seated and recalcitrant; a well-meaning outsider would be able to do little to shift it from its ancient moorings. As Jamie might put it, this was not the best of ideas.

But she had said that she would help, and she would at least try. She had to.

'This other young man,' she began. 'Could you tell me about him? Where did they meet?'

Bruce and Laura exchanged glances. For a few moments, neither spoke. Then Laura said, 'University. He and Richard were students together – here in Edinburgh. They both studied Scottish history. They became friends right at the beginning, I think.'

Isabel noticed that Bruce had lowered his eyes, and it occurred to her that there was another dimension altogether to any animosity between father and son. Of course; of course. This may not be a political difference at all, but an objection to something that was more than a simple friendship. If that were the case, then it would be even more inappropriate for her to get involved. It was not always easy for parents to accept the situation if their offspring came out as gay; things had improved, and it was certainly easier than it used to be, but there was no point in denying that for some parents it was an emotionally difficult issue.

'Close friends?' she asked.

Bruce looked up sharply. It was as if he resented the question.

Laura replied. 'Richard was never interested in other boys,' she said. 'If that's what you're suggesting.' She waited briefly before continuing, 'Anyway, neither Bruce nor I would have a problem with that.'

She looked at Bruce, as if expecting confirmation. He hesitated, Isabel thought – but only briefly – before nodding his agreement. But Isabel was not entirely convinced. They were not telling the truth, she decided.

'It really is political,' said Laura. 'Or that's how it manifests itself – this influence I mentioned. It's as if Richard has become a member of one of those religions that turns you against everybody ...'

'Who isn't a member of the same religion,' Bruce supplied. 'You know the sort. Those fanatical sects that won't eat with anybody else, or even speak to them. That think that everybody who's not with them is fair game.'

'Exactly,' said Laura. 'And it's very painful when you realise that it's his own family he's writing off in this way – his own father.'

Bruce sighed. 'I never expected him to agree with me on everything. It's not as if I ever forced any beliefs down his throat.'

'We never did that,' Laura interjected. 'We let them form their own opinions – within reason, of course.'

'Yes, within reason,' said Bruce. 'You can't bring your children up to believe in *nothing*.'

'Did you discuss politics with them?' asked Isabel. 'The subject must have come up from time to time, I imagine.'

Laura and Bruce exchanged glances. She spoke. 'Not really. Maybe occasionally, I suppose – indirectly. We might have passed some comment on a politician now and then – but

83

nothing much, really. We aren't a very political family, you see. Neither of us is a member of a party, or anything like that.'

'But you have your views?'

It was Bruce who answered. 'Of course we do. But we don't burden others with those opinions. We keep them to ourselves – mostly.'

Isabel nodded. 'But Richard would know how you felt about things?'

At first, neither seemed keen to answer. Then Bruce said, 'I think so. But he'd also know that we expect people to be tolerant of other people's convictions. I would very much hope he knows that.'

'Oh, he does,' said Laura. 'He knows that all right. It's Paul who's somehow persuaded him that tolerance counts for nothing.'

Isabel asked about Paul. Had they had much to do with him? When had his influence come to bear on Richard? Laura explained that they'd been aware that he and Richard were friends, but it was only after they'd both graduated that Richard had seemed to come under his friend's spell. Then, rather quickly, relations had broken down. Richard had accused his father of indifference to Scotland's cause, and this had shortly been followed by a freezing-over of relations. 'And all the time,' she said, 'I can just imagine Paul, smirking in the background, egging him on – filling his head with this stuff.'

'If I could get my hands on that young man ...' muttered Bruce.

Laura corrected him sharply. 'You don't mean that.' And then, turning to Isabel, she said, 'It's very difficult for Bruce. He used to have a very good relationship with Richard.'

Isabel glanced at Bruce. He looked embarrassed. 'It's just that ...' He trailed off.

84

Laura reached for the teapot. 'They live together now,' she said.

'They share a flat,' Bruce said quickly.

Isabel asked where.

Laura pointed vaguely out of the window. 'Down near the canal. They're both keen rowers. It's handy for that.'

'And does Richard have a job?'

'He has a wine shop,' said Bruce. 'You probably know it. It's in Bruntsfield – Holy Corner Wines. Richard bought it with some money his grandmother left him. It's nothing to do with us, though. Our family business, you see, is wine importation. We've been in it for generations.'

Laura explained that they had expected Richard to go into the business, but he had declined to do so.

'He won't work with me,' Bruce said.

Or vice versa, Isabel thought.

'Paul works there too,' Laura said. 'We don't know much about him, other than that they were students together.'

'Actually,' Bruce interjected, 'we've never met Paul.'

Laura explained, 'Richard has never offered to introduce us. I've heard a bit about him from Richard, but not much – even though we own the flat that Richard lives in.'

'He doesn't invite us,' said Bruce.

Laura glanced at her husband. 'No,' she said. 'There have been no invitations.' She paused. 'Paul's from Inverness, I think, but I'm not sure. Stephanie said that his father is a farmer up there.'

'Richard told her that?' asked Isabel. 'Do she and her brother . . .'

'Talk to one another?' Laura shook her head. 'He used to talk to his sister, but now he doesn't. Oh, they'll exchange a few words out of politeness, but it doesn't go further than that.'

'He disapproves of her?'

Laura was about to answer, but Bruce intervened. 'Stephanie's fiancé is English. He must have said something about Scottish politics that Richard took objection to. There was a dreadful argument, I believe, and that led to a souring of relations.' He looked at Isabel, as if uncertain whether to add to what he had said. Then, 'The truth of the matter is—'

'No,' said Laura. 'That's not it, Bruce.'

'It is. It is. The truth of the matter is that he doesn't like him *because* he's English. He's picked that up from Paul. That sort of attitude is infectious. It's a virus. Breathe it in and you catch it.'

'Oh, darling,' Laura protested. 'You've no evidence of that.'

'I've all the evidence I need,' Bruce shot back. 'There are plenty of people in this world who don't like others because of what they happen to be. Greeks and Turks, for instance. Are you telling me that they've always been friends? There are a hundred other national animosities. This tribe dislikes that tribe because of something that happened a long time ago. Or because they needed somebody to dislike and these others were available for the purpose. Or because this set of people believes in one interpretation of history and that set believes in another one altogether. Look at the Balkans. Look anywhere. Sunni and Shia. Take your pick.'

Isabel sighed. He was right. The world was a patchwork of animosities: hate had a hundred different flavours, and its sinister salesmen knew all about marketing. And the point about such feelings was that once they took hold, they ran deep. 'You know,' she said, 'I really don't see that I'll be able to do very much here. Oil can always be poured on troubled waters, but . . . ' She sighed again.

Laura seemed not to have noticed her reservations. 'Just find out a bit more about this young man who's influencing him.

And maybe talk to Richard. Tell him that his father loves him very much,' she urged. 'Tell him that. He won't take it from me. Somebody outside the family has to try to get through to him. For us, it's like trying to talk to somebody who's on a different wavelength.'

Wavelengths, thought Isabel, were a useful metaphor. If you shared a wavelength with somebody then you would find it easy to talk. You would be comfortable in their company and there would be no intrusive static, no distortion. It was like that between her and Jamie; it always had been. Sometimes, in fact, she felt they hardly needed speech at all, but could say everything through looks and gestures, or even through something which might be called telepathy, which did not exist, the physicists told us, and yet which seemed to surprise us from time to time with a telephone call coming in just as we thought of somebody and knew, even before we answered, who it would be. Coincidence ... yes, of course it was that, and nothing more; we could not start to believe in things for which there was no evidence, because if we started to believe in one such thing, even if it was harmless, then there was nothing to stop the siren call of other, more harmful beliefs. And if we dismantled science, and scientific notions of observable cause and effect, then what certainty would we have of anything?

She and Jamie were on the same wavelength – there was no doubt about that – but Cat was another matter altogether. Cat *thought* differently, Isabel sometimes felt. And although they could talk to one another, they sometimes meant different things by the same words. That was a common issue, and it cropped up in all sorts of circumstances – including, she thought, right here in this Edinburgh house, with its neat garden and its air of solidity and correctness – under this roof there had been a misunderstanding as to what the word

Scotland meant. For a father, it meant one thing, and for a son it appeared to mean another. And that difference could be extrapolated to cover so many cases where there was a difference of opinion. She thought of her cousin in Mobile for whom the word *America* meant something quite different from what it meant to her cousin in Dallas. They both believed in the good – neither was malicious in her temperament – but when they used the same words, they were often talking about radically different things.

'Different wavelengths?' said Isabel. 'Yes, I know what you mean.'

Laura clasped her hands together – the body language of entreaty. 'We've heard, from several people, that you have a gift for sorting things out for people. They all say the same thing. That's why we've asked you.'

Isabel thought: I have no alternative. Then she went on to think: strictly speaking, that isn't true – there is the thing you can do, which may be the rational, sensible thing to do, and then there is the thing you *must* do because none of us is entirely rational and sensible, however much we might like to be. So she had no choice, in a manner of speaking.

'I'll do what I can,' she said.

As she said this, she thought: this is ridiculous. Here am I agreeing to barge into a family mess that I shall probably only make worse. This is none of my business. It is not a complicated situation – it is really quite simple. A young man has broken away from his conventionally minded family. He has gone off with a friend whom the parents cannot accept because they do not want their son to be what his nature prompts him to be. They are doing exactly what they should *not* do in such a case, and are losing him. The quickest way to lose one's children was to fail to accept the person with whom they want to spend their lives: any number of fractured families were evidence of that. In this case, they're blaming his friend; they're blaming his political views; they're accusing him of intolerance when they themselves are lacking in tolerance.

Then she thought: perhaps not. Perhaps what they say is correct, and Richard has been mindnapped. Was there such a word? There should be, she thought

7

'You go first,' said Jamie, as he sliced the raw potato that would shortly be transformed into potato dauphinoise, the dish that, were it entirely up to him, they would have, if not every day, then at least several times a week.

'Potato dauphinoise?' said Isabel from behind a small pile of unopened mail stacked on the kitchen table.

Jamie was apologetic. '*Faute de mieux,*' he said.

Isabel reached for an envelope and slit it open with a kitchen knife. *For want of something better.* You could not airily say *faute de mieux* as if it were a justification, because it was generally simply not true: more often than not, there *would* be something better. But now, with Jamie doing the cooking on an evening when it was really her turn, but when he had said that she looked tired and he would do it instead, you could not quibble about the chosen menu. The potato dauphinoise would be served with anchovies and a walnut salad – she could already smell the anchovies and see the salad ingredients – and she knew the result would be perfect and she had nothing to complain about. The mail, which seemed to consist mostly of catalogues, along with a couple of magazines, was undemanding; her glass of chilled elderflower cordial was in front of her; and the boys, who had been exhausted by the time they were put to bed, were soundly asleep. In such circumstances, potato dauphinoise and walnut salad could hardly be improved upon. Jamie was wrong: it was not *faute de mieux*.

She glanced at a catalogue she had extracted from its envelope. It was from a firm that produced fabric from recycled plastic bottles. Six hundred plastic water bottles, the catalogue explained, would produce a rectangular, pastel-coloured throw (as illustrated). She looked at the picture. She had ordered such a throw several months ago and she knew that the catalogue's claims were entirely correct: it was impossible to tell – by touch at least – the difference between the material they produced and real wool. It was, Isabel thought, a highly unlikely miracle of chemistry. How could a plastic bottle, smooth and brittle, be turned into something warm and soft? She would order one of their small rugs next, because their alchemy extended to making floor coverings too, and they could do with something for the downstairs bathroom, where the floor was cold to bare feet.

Now Jamie said, once again, 'You go first.' He had started to grate cheese – Gruyère, by the look of it, which she loved, almost as much as Parmesan.

She put the catalogue aside and began to tell him about her day, starting with the conversation with Cat and then moving on to the visit to Laura Douglas and her husband. Jamie, who was now chopping a red pepper, looked up from his task. To her surprise, he was grinning.

'Where angels fear to tread,' he said.

'I had hoped you might have some ideas,' she said.

He shook his head as he mixed the strips of red pepper into the salad. 'All right: he's had enough of his family. He wants a bit of freedom. No surprises there.'

'Possibly not,' said Isabel.

'So he's picked a position that puts him as far as possible away from them – and what they stand for.'

'Which is what?' asked Isabel. She thought that Jamie had rather prejudged the Douglases, whom he did not know. 'What do you imagine they stand for?'

'The existing order. The boat that he thinks needs to be rocked. That's what people usually think their parents stand for.'

'And the friend? How does he fit into it?'

Jamie shrugged. 'He could be a boyfriend. He probably is. I doubt if he's behind all this; he's just the catalyst.'

Isabel sighed. 'So, what do I do?'

Jamie stood back from the salad and seemed to be contemplating his handiwork. 'You could tell them that you've considered your position and there really is nothing you can do.' He glanced at her; it was obvious that she would not do this. 'Or you could go to see this guy. What's his name?'

'Richard.'

'You go to see Richard and you tell him that he's upsetting his parents and that there's no need to be so brutal about it. You tell him he's more than made his point.'

'And then?'

'I imagine nothing much will happen. But he might just get the message. People sometimes do. He might just relent a bit. I'm not sure, though. It can take years for people to forgive their parents. Years. And some people never do.'

Of course, thought Isabel. And then she wondered what Charlie and Magnus would have to forgive. Was that the goal of parenthood: to ensure that your children had as little to forgive as possible?

'And then suddenly,' Jamie continued, 'our parents are no longer there and we're into posthumous apology territory.'

She thought: yes, the desire to say sorry doesn't end when those who have been wronged are no longer there; it could even become stronger, as it did with slavery, that great historical wrong that had returned, almost unexpectedly, to haunt those who thought it had nothing to do with them. There were other wrongs, too, almost too many to enumerate, because there were infinite ways in which humanity could be unkind to itself.

She became decisive. 'I'll go and see him,' she said.

Jamie looked thoughtful. 'You might find out a bit more about his friend,' he mused. 'Before you speak to Richard, that is.'

'Do you think so?'

'Yes. It might be useful to know what you're up against.' He paused before adding, 'Just an idea.'

Isabel considered this, but did not commit herself. She wanted to ask Jamie about his day. He had been in rehearsal and then put in a spell teaching at the Academy. He often had stories about what one of his pupils had said or done, or some snippet of gossip from the staffroom. One of his colleagues was involved in a neighbourhood dispute and had been entertaining Jamie with the latest news from the tenement. The argument had shifted to responsibility for the changing of a light bulb on the stair. This task required a longer ladder than any of the proprietors possessed, but nobody was prepared to buy one, some even being reluctant to pay a contribution to the cost. This issue had been reported on for weeks now without any apparent likelihood of resolution.

'Ladder news?' she asked.

Jamie smiled. 'That's been sorted,' he said. 'They got hold of a man with a ladder – an electrician. They had to pay his bill, of course, but there's a principle involved in these things. But—' He broke off while he mixed the salad dressing. Isabel waited. She picked up the catalogue and found herself thinking again of the process by which wool, or something that seemed to have all the properties of wool, was extracted from plastic detritus. It was chemistry, of course, rather than alchemy, even if it looked more like the latter than the former.

'But there's something going on in the orchestra.'

Isabel looked up. Jamie had recently been given a part-time seat in a newly established chamber orchestra. The orchestra's funding had at first been precarious, but it had recently managed to attract a generous commercial patron thanks to the efforts of its fundraiser. For Jamie it was an ideal job – one that was not too demanding in terms of time, but that gave him the opportunity to work with first-rank players.

'I told you about our conductor, didn't I?' asked Jamie.

Isabel tried to remember what he had said. She had not been paying particular attention when he had described his first rehearsal with the orchestra; he had said something about the conductor, whom he disliked for some reason – or distrusted, perhaps.

'You did,' she said. 'But I'm afraid I've forgotten what you told me.'

'He's very tall – which is an irrelevant detail, of course.'

Not really, thought Isabel: irrelevant details could be part of the overall picture. Tall men might, just might, behave differently from short men. She thought of the tall men she had known. Were they noticeably different from the short men she had known – in any respect, other than height? Were tall men gentler, on the whole, having less to prove? Or was that just a popular – and unfounded – misconception? She thought it was.

There must be something else. She waved a hand. What was he? A bit bossy, was it? But then was that not exactly what conductors should be? There would be no point in having a conductor who failed to tell the orchestra what to do. *In your own time . . .* or *Play this as you see fit* were hardly instructions expected of a conductor.

'He's a bit of a flirt,' said Jamie. 'He thinks he's God's gift to women.'

Isabel remembered now. Jamie had said that the conductor could not take his eyes off an attractive flautist who was standing in for somebody else at a rehearsal. He had explained how this could lead to confusion in a setting where, if the conductor looked at you, it was because he was expecting you to do something particular – to emphasise a passage in the work, for instance, or to give a previously agreed interpretation to the score.

'You told me about that,' Isabel said.

'Well, it's worse than I thought,' said Jamie.

Isabel winced. This would be another case of unwanted attention. It was something that women had endured for a long time but were now exposing and resisting. It was an uncomfortable process, but such conduct was unacceptable. Talking about it was not always easy for the victims, but people had to learn they could not get away with it.

'Is he making it difficult for somebody?' she asked.

To her surprise, Jamie shook his head.

'No, it's nothing like that. Not all attention's unwelcome. But I think – well a few of us think – that there's something going on.'

This was not very informative. *Something's going on . . .* There was always something going on if one looked hard enough. Isabel encouraged him. 'What, exactly?'

Jamie had been standing as he prepared their meal. Now he sat down and poured himself a glass of wine, ignoring the jug of elderflower on the table. He was a fitness enthusiast and hence a light drinker, often pouring himself no more than half a glass; Isabel could manage two, but usually left it at that. Wine, she thought, tasted quite different after the second glass. Watching him now, pouring the wine almost up to the brim, Isabel decided that Jamie was upset.

'All right,' he said. 'Let me tell you what I think. I may be wrong about it, but I don't think I am. I think I'm right.'

Isabel inclined her head. 'I'm sure you are.'

'Well, you never know,' said Jamie. 'Sometimes we think we're right, but we're wrong. Even you . . . ' He hesitated, but Isabel made it easy for him.

'Oh, I get it spectacularly wrong,' she admitted. 'Sometimes. In fact, rather often.'

He demurred. 'Not more than anybody else, I imagine.'

She thanked him. He was, as usual, being kind. That was one of the reasons – just one – why she loved him so much. He was kind. She could not imagine being married to somebody who was capable of unkindness. How could one love somebody who was vicious – in the strict, philosophical sense of the term, afflicted with vice? And yet there were plenty of people who did precisely that, she thought, who loved the unlovable. The vilest of men had wives and partners who loved them. Mafia bosses and war criminals, torturers and serial killers, often had somebody who loved them in spite of everything. And they had mothers, too, who often failed to give up on them even in the face of overwhelming evidence of their son's misdeeds. *I know it looks as if he did all those nasty things, but I really don't think he'd do that – not my son.* The world understood, of course, and would never expect a mother to recognise her son for what he was, even if, occasionally, that was what a mother did.

'Tell me,' Isabel prompted. 'Tell me what this conductor—'

'Laurence. He's called Laurence. He doesn't like being called Larry.'

Isabel thought there was a difference. If she were a Laurence, she would not want to be a Larry either.

Jamie continued, 'Laurence doesn't like the system that the board – the orchestra's board – have put in place. They got hold of a democratic model for orchestral governance – or that's what they called it. They pulled that out of their hat and applied it. It insists that certain important decisions have to be ratified by the players themselves, or even be made collectively.'

'Decisions as to what to play?' asked Isabel. 'Does everyone have a say in that?'

Jamie looked rueful. 'No, not that. It's a nice idea, but I doubt if it would work. People disagree too much on that.' He thought of the particular composer he did not like, against whom he would vote – to register a protest, if for no other reason. But then he imagined what Isabel might say if he expressed such sentiments, and he put the thought aside. Being married to Isabel had many positive features, but it also involved a form of moral self-scrutiny that could be demanding. But Jamie would not have it otherwise. She was the woman he adored, and if he was being influenced by her – which he was – then there was nobody else by whom he would rather be swayed.

'And it's a matter of pride for many musicians,' he continued, 'that they can play whatever's put in front of them. Some people enjoy playing music they can't stand. They like the challenge.

No, it's not the day-to-day things that are affected: it's major decisions that need to be made – or endorsed – by everyone. Such as appointments. Who gets the job, in other words.'

Isabel guessed what was coming. 'He wanted to give somebody a job? Without anybody else being involved in the selection process?' That, she thought, was an old story.

Jamie nodded. 'Yes. That's exactly it.'

'And there are people in the orchestra who think he's trying to push a particular candidate—'

Jamie interrupted her. 'How do you know what I'm going to say?'

Isabel smiled. 'Second sight? A great-aunt – on my father's side – was a Highlander. They're very interested in that sort of thing up there. They talk about people being *fey*. That's having the ability to see what's coming.'

'A useful gift,' said Jamie.

'They kept asking her to predict the results of horse races,' Isabel said. 'She refused. But then they saw her going into a betting shop up in Inverness and coming out with a broad smile on her face.'

Jamie laughed. 'Of course, there was the Brahan Seer – that man up in Easter Ross. He was said to have second sight in a big way. And his predictions have been shown to be true.'

Isabel's natural scepticism asserted itself. She had not been serious about second sight. 'I doubt it,' she said. 'People read all sorts of things into Nostradamus. We're a gullible species.'

Jamie was not so sure. 'We may be gullible, but look at the facts.'

'Which are?'

'The Brahan Seer lived at the beginning of the seventeenth century, right?'

'Something like that.'

'Well, he did,' said Jamie. 'And yet he seemed to predict the Battle of Culloden, which was in 1745. And the Second World War.'

Isabel looked doubtful.

'But he did,' protested Jamie. 'He was quite specific. He said that a new parliament would be opened in Edinburgh when men could walk dry-shod from England to France. That's the tunnel under the English Channel, I would have thought. When was that opened? 1994. And when was the Scottish Parliament reconvened in Edinburgh for the first time after the Act of Union? A few years after that.'

'That could be coincidence,' said Isabel.

'And the Second World War?' Jamie insisted. 'He said that when there were five bridges over the River Ness, there would be widespread chaos in Europe. The fifth bridge was completed in August 1939. Another coincidence?'

Isabel shrugged. 'Possibly. Possibly not. I suppose I remain agnostic about these things. And anyway, wasn't there some doubt as to whether he actually existed?'

Jamie looked deflated. 'The Brahan Seer? Who says he didn't exist?'

Isabel shrugged. 'I seem to recall reading somewhere or other that there are no records of anybody who could have been him.'

Jamie looked thoughtful. 'Perhaps one should keep an open mind.'

Isabel agreed. 'Yes, you're right. I don't believe in second sight, but that's not to say that second sight doesn't exist. It may, for all we know – whether or not I believe in it.' She paused. 'How did we get onto this?'

'I said you seemed able to work out what I was going to say.'

'Of course. I can't work it out, you know. But . . .'

'But what?'

'But,' Isabel went on, 'if you were to ask me what was coming next, I'd probably say that it was this: your conductor is giving a job to a lover.'

Jamie stared at her, and she knew immediately that she was right.

'I'm just deducing that,' she said, rather weakly. 'I don't *know* it.'

'Well, it's true. That's exactly what's happening. Or what we strongly suspect is going to happen.'

Isabel said that there was nothing particularly new about a job being allocated on the basis of personal friendship. It was not meant to happen, but it inevitably did.

'We don't like it,' said Jamie. 'Apparently there's a much better player who's not going to get it because Laurence wanted his candidate to get the job.'

'But can't the players object? You said that these decisions were meant to be democratic. This sounds anything but that.'

Jamie explained that the board had specifically authorised the conductor to choose the new player himself. It was a special circumstance, it said, because there was no time to involve everybody in the decision.

'And that's what has happened?'

'Almost, but not quite. Laurence advertised the post and arranged for auditions. He invited one of violinists to conduct the auditions with him. They've auditioned six players. Three were turned down the same day – three were kept on the shortlist. One of these three is by far the most talented. She's won all sorts of prizes. She's recorded with impressive labels. But she's not going to get it, I think.'

Isabel asked him how he knew.

'The whole business has been leaky,' said Jamie. 'The

violinist he chose as the orchestra's representative, so to speak, is somebody we call the Mouse. He's really timid. He wouldn't say boo to a goose. He was window-dressing, put there to tick the consultation box, and he'll be completely in the palm of Laurence's hand.'

Isabel took a sip of her elderflower. This was corruption. It was a familiar, sleazy story, and it always depressed her. It was endemic. Sometimes it seemed to be an inevitable concomitant of human nature. You chopped off one Medusa-like head of corruption, and several more sprouted almost immediately. It was bleak. 'And the person who's getting the job? Tell me about her.'

Jamie said that she had not yet been appointed. There were to be further auditions for the three players on the shortlist, and these would not take place for another three weeks. But the Mouse had let slip that the post would be filled by a young woman called Athene, whatever should happen at the auditions. 'The Mouse is friendly with our bass player. She's called Jill. She's kind to the Mouse. Anyway, she was in the pub with the Mouse after a rehearsal – the Mouse drinks lemonade shandies – and he suddenly confided in her that the whole thing was a stitch-up. Annette Jamieson – the really good player – was not going to get the job because Laurence was going to give it to this woman called Athene. He said this, and then apparently he clammed up. Jill told everybody.'

'And you're sure there's a relationship between Laurence and Athene?' asked Isabel.

'Yes. Somebody saw them having lunch together at The Chaumer in Queen Street. You know that place? A pianist I know said that she has seen them more than once on Fridays. Just the two of them. It looks as if they have a regular date.'

Isabel wondered whether that constituted proof of a

relationship.

'Probably,' said Jamie, then, seeing Isabel's doubtful look, added, 'I'd say so, anyway.'

After a few moments she asked, 'What are you going to do about it?'

Jamie hesitated. When he answered, it was in a slightly sheepish tone. 'I don't feel like ignoring it.'

Isabel said it was not something that should be ignored. 'People shouldn't get away with that sort of thing.' She paused. Jamie was looking at her expectantly.

Suddenly, a smile broke across her face. 'A few moments ago, you said that I could tell what you were about to say.'

'Yes,' he said. 'I did.' And then he added, 'I wasn't entirely serious, of course. I don't believe in telepathy.'

'Well, right now you're about to ask me whether I could do something about this.'

He stared at her blankly. Then he shook his head. 'No, not really. I mean, almost . . . You see, I was going to do something myself. I was going to . . . ' He shrugged. He was not sure what he was intending to do.

Isabel came to his rescue. 'Here's an idea, Jamie. I'll see if I can do something about what's going on in your orchestra if you, in turn . . . ' She waved a hand in the air.

He understood, and could not conceal his surprise. 'You want me to speak to Richard Douglas?'

'Yes,' said Isabel. She had not planned this sudden exchange, but now that she came to think about it, it seemed to her to be perfectly reasonable. There was no harm, she thought, in Jamie's finding out how complicated and demanding her life could be. Stepping into the shoes of another was the best way of establishing and understanding how the world was for other people. That, after all, was how moral imagination was formed: you experienced what the other experienced and learned from it.

Jamie hesitated for a few moments before he replied. Then he said, 'All right.'

Isabel was pleased. Her sense of fairness had been offended by the story Jamie had told her and it would give her satisfaction to do something about it. She knew that this is what Jamie wanted, but would not necessarily be able to achieve. He lacked her experience of dealing with situations like this, but for her, it was nothing particularly new and she saw no reason why a few well-placed enquiries on her part would not give them enough ammunition to deal with Laurence and his machinations. She had done similar things before, and there was nothing to suggest that this enquiry would be any different. Human misdeeds, after all, were all the same, no matter the context in which they were performed. They inevitably had the same miserable footprint, the same banality, the same grubby features. There was nothing new about wrongdoing, nothing new about it at all – especially when it came to sex and its ability to dull the moral sense, confuse our every compass, and lead us to do things that we knew we really should not do.

Of course Laurence knew he should not give a job to his lover; of course he knew that it was wrong to pass over a highly qualified candidate; but neither of these would stop him from obeying the promptings of sexual desire. That desire had a potency all its own, and sometimes it took a saint to resist. Laurence, by all accounts, was no saint; he was a mortal conductor with a mortal lover and an obvious ability to compartmentalise his conscience. He was, thought Isabel, a man, with all the failings of a man. She reminded herself that Jamie was a man too, but he was a man unlike any she had met before. He was gentle, considerate, good-looking, understanding, intelligent, artistic. He was everything any woman could possibly want in a man. Laurence, she imagined, was none of that. But then she thought: how can I think that when I've never even met him? Of course we judge people we do not know – we do that regularly – but I'm not going to do that, Isabel thought. I'm going to give Laurence a chance. Just because Jamie doesn't like him, there's no reason for me to do the same. There was no point in being a philosopher – which she was – and then allowing yourself to be swayed by prejudice.

Jamie was looking at her. He smiled at her fondly. 'You're very beautiful,' he said.

She smiled. 'Flatterer,' she whispered.

He took a few steps towards her. He bent down. He kissed her.

8

Isabel's two boys, Charlie and Magnus, were now both in the early years of their schooling. Magnus, the younger of the two, had until recently been at a nursery round the corner from the house – a noisy, cheerful place presided over by twin sisters: the Misses Robinson, as they called themselves. Charlie, being slightly older, had been enrolled in the pre-school year of George Watson's College, a block or two further away, and was now promoted to the first year of primary school while Magnus took his place in the pre-school year.

Watson's was a highly regarded school that took children from four to eighteen, and was known, among other things, for its pipe band. Isabel's route to the classrooms took her past the hall in the school grounds where, at that time of the morning, the pipe band practised. She listened to its progress over the school term, and came to anticipate the pipe tunes that were associated with particular mornings. On Fridays, for some reason, the piping tutor seemed to have a preference for 'Mist-Covered Mountains' and 'Lochaber No More'; on Mondays, again for no discernible reason, 'A Scottish Soldier' would be played by the whole band, complete with enthusiastic drumming. Charlie would stick his fingers in his ears and grimace as they walked past. 'You can join that later, Charlie,' Isabel shouted to him above the sound of the pipes. 'When you're bigger, that is.'

'Won't,' said Charlie, scowling.

'You don't have to, of course. But it would be nice to play the pipes, don't you think?'

'Won't,' repeated Charlie.

Isabel smiled at him. 'The boys and girls who play the pipes have a very good time,' she said. 'Listen to them.'

Charlie shook his head. 'Won't,' he said a third time.

She did not press the matter. She had been discussing music lessons with a friend who was a music teacher, and she had advised her not to push either of the boys into playing a musical instrument until they were ready to do so of their own accord.

'You can put them off for life,' her friend said. 'It's like forcing children to eat something they don't like. They can end up hating whatever it is for the rest of their days. Whereas if you give them time, they can come round.'

Isabel thought about this. He was right. She knew somebody who had been obliged to eat pineapple as a child and was now repelled by it. Nobody should be forced to eat pineapple, she thought, and yet she was not sure whether children could be left to embrace things of their own free will. How many children learned the piano without being obliged to practise their scales? Surely musicianship was like any of the other skills that we taught children, sometimes against their will, and then, later on, they thanked us for it. Did Mozart ever thank Leopold Mozart for seating him at the piano when he was barely able

106

to sit unsupported? Or had he climbed up onto the stool of his own volition? Isabel knew that opinion was divided on that, with some biographers painting Leopold as an oppressive tyrant, and others seeing him as a wise counterbalance to a wilful and unreliable son.

'People make fun of pushy mothers,' Isabel once observed to Jamie. 'But if we didn't have pushy mothers, we wouldn't have anybody – anybody at all – who could play the piano. You have to do it.'

'Have to do what?' Jamie asked.

'You have to make them practise. You have to stand over them and make them. If you don't, they won't do it.'

Jamie looked doubtful. 'Nobody forced me to play.'

'Are you sure?' she asked.

'Yes, I'm sure. I had to nag my parents to buy me a bassoon. They never *made* me play.'

Isabel thought about this. 'You probably had to put pressure on them to buy a bassoon because they're such expensive instruments.'

Jamie still looked doubtful.

'Actually,' Isabel continued, 'the issue is much bigger than bassoons and so on. It's one of how much freedom you give children to decide for themselves.' She paused. 'It can be about religion. Should we give our children our beliefs – or lack of beliefs – or let them choose for themselves later on?'

It was a question to which recently they had both given some thought. Charlie had asked about God a few days before, and Jamie had found himself embarrassed by the question. Children always asked the obvious theological question about where God lived, and Charlie had asked just that, although he had appended to this a subsidiary question about whether God needed to go to the bathroom. Jamie had reported this conversation to Isabel, who had burst out laughing. 'Of course that's an obvious question to a child. In fact, a child who *didn't* ask that would be missing something.' She asked Jamie how he had responded.

'I changed the subject,' he said. 'That's what you do with a question you don't know how to answer. Ask any politician. I know I should have tried to answer him, but . . . but I didn't.'

'And what did you say?'

Jamie hesitated. 'I said the first thing that came into my mind. I told him that there used to be wolves in Scotland.'

She stared at him. 'Wolves? What's that got to do with it?'

He shrugged. 'Nothing. But I wanted to divert him.'

Isabel looked incredulous. 'And did it?'

'Oh yes. He stopped asking about God going to the bathroom. He went straight into wolves. He seemed to have learned something about how dogs were descended from wolves – heaven knows where he got it from. Pre-school, I suppose.'

'They have to teach them something,' said Isabel wryly. She still felt that he should have answered Charlie. 'You might have replied to his question,' she said.

He gave her a challenging look. 'What if I didn't know the answer?'

Isabel thought of a more important dimension to this discussion. She and Jamie had never talked about that most fundamental of issues: whether they believed in a god. They had married in Canongate Kirk and had exchanged their marriage vows there before their friend, Iain Torrance, but that did not mean that either of them had a developed theology. She knew that Jamie was not hostile to religious belief, but did he actually believe in a supreme being, whatever identity he might give to such a notion? And more critically, what were her own views on the subject? She was a philosopher, but being a philosopher had never required her to sit down and work out exactly what she felt about this issue. She felt there might be something beyond us, beyond the material, but she was not sure about giving that a precise and defined identity. If she listened to Orthodox chanting – as she occasionally liked to do – then she found herself open to the spirituality that underpinned such things. Similarly, if she saw religion in action in the world, in the face of suffering or distress – when religion might be the only available agent of solace or comfort – then she could not help but be moved by what she saw. But could she bring herself to believe in the dogmatic claims of religion? The virgin birth? Original sin? There she felt a real doubt, especially when religions said that they were right and everybody else was wrong. That was anathema to her. There was such a thing as the spiritual impulse, she felt; and many of us felt the need to connect with a world of spirit, but how could anybody claim that their particular response to this was somehow privileged, was true, while others, feeling the same impulse, were simply wrong? So when the Christian church claimed, as some branches of it still did, that the only route into the divine presence was through its specific rituals, or by an acceptance of its particular claims, then she parted company with such a narrow and exclusive view of the world.

Perhaps she should not worry too much about this, of course, because it was no longer necessary to believe in any particular chapter and verse – nowadays what counted was the spiritual impulse behind the outer forms, the rituals, the profession of a faith. And if one believed in something beyond our material world, then it didn't matter what name one gave to that being. Nor what gender that being was. Or its location. And it was certainly not necessary to believe that such a being needed to be placated. That was straight out of ancient Greek beliefs in vengeful gods and it sat ill with modern views of what God might be.

Jamie was asking her a question. 'And do we have a position on this?'

She smiled. 'On the bathroom issue? I would have thought we don't exactly *need* to consider that one.'

'About where he lives.'

Isabel thought for a moment. He was right, she thought. Parents should try to present a united front – at least on important issues – and the parenting manuals were agreed on the need to avoid confusing the child with conflicting signals. That meant you could not have one parent saying that bedtime was seven and another saying it was eight. You could not have one parent indulging a child while another denied him or her. But did that apply to theological questions too?

'No,' she said, in reply to Jamie. 'I don't think we do. I think we might leave the question until later.'

Jamie looked dubious. 'Dodge it?'

She looked away. 'Perhaps we should give him some very general answers. We can tell him that God is all about us. And leave it at that.'

'Unless we want to bring him up as an atheist.' He fixed her with a stare. It seemed to her that he was undecided, and wanted her guidance.

'I'm not sure.' She felt uncomfortable. 'I would like to have a faith. I'd like to believe in a world in which there is some purpose. I'd like to believe that there is something precious in each and every one of us – something that has a value, a meaning, beyond our petty human concerns.' She paused. 'Is that sentimental? Is that wishful thinking?'

He shook his head. 'I don't think so.'

'And I think that sometimes we need to have a set of beliefs — myths, if you want to call them that — that allow us to feel the things I've just mentioned; that give us a language to express the sense of value.'

He nodded. 'I understand what you mean.'

'Because we have to act together,' Isabel went on. 'If we are to combat the things that are wrong in this world, we have to act together. And religious belief — as long as it's benevolent — enables us to do that.'

She stopped. She was not sure if that was right. People could rally to a secular banner just as enthusiastically as they could to a religious one. *Aux armes, citoyens* . . . And yet, secular banners could quickly become threadbare and tatty, just as they might be used to intimidate or repress. Religion, of course, had nothing to learn when it came to repression . . . She sighed. There was, she thought, a kernel of truth somewhere in all our theological speculation — a spark that was worth encouraging, that could inspire us to tackle things that would otherwise defeat or discourage us.

She made another attempt. 'If we're children lost in the dark — and sometimes that's exactly what we are . . .'

Jamie nodded. 'I agree. We are. And it *is* dark.'

'Then by joining hands with one another,' Isabel continued, 'we give ourselves the necessary courage to fight the battle we know we're going to have to fight.'

He was silent.

She suddenly thought of people who were sustained by faith and who, apparently *post hoc, ergo propter hoc*, did good in their lives. There was a man she knew, a member of the Community of the Resurrection, an Anglican order, who devoted his time to helping young people in an African country beset by incorrigible economic failure. He tirelessly solicited funds to

111

buy children school textbooks and clothing. He found them places to live. He rescued stunted young lives and gave them the light that would help them grow. And he did this every day, unremittingly, while the sophisticates – who raised an eyebrow at monasticism, who would have regarded his faith as irrational, wishful thinking – did nothing. He made a difference to scores of lives. He might have done that out of the goodness of his heart even if he did not have his religious faith, but would simple goodness of heart, unstructured around community and tradition, get one up at six in the morning to begin to look after others?

She decided to persist. 'That means that most of us are going to need to be part of a communion of belief of some sort. It could be religious belief or lay belief – either energises us. It gives us the strength we might otherwise never have.' You had to believe in something, she thought, or you simply would not act. That was inescapably true. If you did not believe it worthwhile to help the weak, then you would not bother to do it. Belief of one sort or another lay at the heart of action.

'No. You're right.'

'So I suggest that we bring up the boys to believe in some-thing – as long as it's not psychologically harmful. And I don't think nurturing a vague belief in a loving god is psychologic-ally harmful. It won't make you treat people any worse – in fact, it will help you, I would have thought, to treat people a bit better.'

Jamie almost said, 'If one needs the prop.' But for some reason he did not. Instead he said, 'And there's nothing wrong with that.' Did it matter, he asked himself, if the stories we told might not be true in the literal sense? What counted was whether they expressed some deeper truth.

She waited to see if there was more that he wanted to say,

but there was not. There were still questions that remained unanswered, but the exchange of ideas between the two of them had been important. Neither had said anything un-equivocal or unambiguous, but each had the sense that they knew a little bit more about what the other believed, or did not believe; or perhaps not. And there was nothing to be ashamed of in that. It was not wishy-washy, it was not cowardly, to fail to pin one's colours to a mast. Sometimes, Isabel felt, the most honest thing to do was to confess that one was not entirely sure; and that uncertainty, even vagueness, was a perfectly defensible position. After all, what had Yeats said? 'The best lack all conviction while the worst are full of passionate intensity.' He seemed to have bemoaned that situation; perhaps he might have celebrated it. Perhaps the best were the best precisely because they were not full of passionate intensity; although I'm not among the best, she thought – by no means. Jamie was, though. She felt convinced of that at least.

On that morning, Isabel was late in getting the children out of the house. Jamie had left early to catch a train to Glasgow, where he was rehearsing with Scottish Opera. They were working on a production of the *Meistersingers*. 'Lots of noise,' he said. 'Lots and lots of it. Bang! Crash!' He liked Wagner because, as he put it, the music washed over you; you could sleep through sections of a Wagner opera, he claimed, half seriously – even if you were in the orchestra. Not that Jamie did that, although at a rehearsal recently an oboist had dozed off and had to be reminded by the conductor that there were still several hundred bars to go.

Without Jamie to assist her, Isabel had to struggle along with both children, carrying Magnus, who was not in a mood to walk, and dragging a reluctant Charlie behind her. Both boys had perked up on entering the school gates – a good sign, Isabel thought – and the walk was thereafter easier. Even so, she was relieved when they reached the entrance to the two side-by-side classrooms and she was able to consign Magnus to the care of a member of the pre-school staff.

'Sausages for lunch today?' asked the assistant, ready to note the preference on a clipboard. 'Or vegetable lasagne with salad?'

Charlie chose for his brother. 'Sausages,' he said.

'Shut up,' snapped Magnus.

Isabel bent down to admonish him. 'That's not a nice thing to say to your brother.'

Magnus made a scatological remark, and laughed.

Isabel glanced apologetically at the assistant. 'I'm sorry,' she said. 'He's at that stage.'

The assistant smiled tolerantly. 'Shall I write down sausages?'

Isabel nodded. 'We love sausages, don't we, Magnus?'

And then she handed him over before a further debate could keep the subject open.

The next gate along was the entrance to Primary One block. Small figures, abandoned at the door by their parents, thronged in the corridor that led to the classrooms. High-pitched voices, raised to produce that constant, cicada-like shriek that accompanies any gathering of young children, provided a backdrop of noise. A couple of teachers, conferring before the start of the school day, lingered near the door. One of these noticed Isabel consigning Charlie to the melee, and gestured for her to stay.

Miss Young was Charlie's teacher. Isabel had been told her first name – was it Jean, or perhaps Jeanie? – but had never progressed beyond the formal description by which parents refer to their offspring's teachers.

'A word with you, Ms Dalhousie, if you don't mind.'

Isabel waited as Miss Young detached herself from her colleague and approached her. She wondered whether she had forgotten to do something she was meant to do. The school was always sending back circulars that asked parents to do this, that, or the next thing. *Please remember to give your child a water bottle. Do not – repeat not – send disposable plastic bottles. Please remember the oceans.* That had annoyed her. As if she would forget the oceans. Or, a note that was occasionally tucked into Charlie's school bag addressed simply to 'Parent', its content free of any conservation message but powerful nonetheless. *There has been a case of nits in Primary One. Please check your child's hair and, in the event of there being any infestation, use one of the preparations available from pharmacies. If you require further information on how to deal with this issue, please arrange to speak to the school nurse, who will demonstrate the use of a nit comb.*

A seditious thought had occurred to Isabel when she first read such a note. Having checked Charlie's hair and found no evidence of the tiny lice, she reflected on the anonymity of the notification. *A case of nits . . .* What if the school were to be more specific? *Nits have been found in the hair of . . .* insert name of child. *It is possible that your child has had contact with this child, or with this child's wider family . . .* That would be a nice touch; guilt, or infection perhaps, by association. What an electric effect that would have. What emotions – shame, suspicion, reproach – would be let loose on the community of parents. Of course, that was ridiculous, but sometimes it was amusing to reflect on things that could never be, to imagine what might happen if a stone – or a boulder in this case – were thrown into the placid surface of respectable Edinburgh life.

Miss Young was looking at her expectantly, and Isabel realised that she had been thinking about head lice. 'I'm sorry,' she said. 'Thoughts elsewhere.'

Miss Young nodded, as if she knew that Isabel had a tangential mental life.

'I said, I'm sorry to raise this with you, but we need to have a wee word about Charlie.'

Isabel drew in her breath. Charlie had been dry for a long time, but sometimes small children had accidents. Was that the problem?

'He's been biting people,' said Miss Young.

It took Isabel a few moments to take this in. Some time ago, when he was still at nursery school, Charlie had been through a spell of biting. She had struggled with that, and had eventually cured it in an old-fashioned way by putting a small dab of mustard in his mouth when he bit Magnus. She had felt guilty about this crude aversion therapy, but it had worked, and Charlie had stopped biting. She had not thought it would recur, but now it seemed that it might have done. Perhaps he had forgotten about the mustard.

She stared at the teacher, trying to collect her thoughts. 'Biting?'

Miss Young nodded patiently. 'Yes. A few days ago he bit Steven. On the leg.'

Isabel's mouth dropped open. She knew Steven, whose father was a member of the Scottish Parliament who had spoken on television recently about street violence. And here was Charlie engaging in exactly that, although the incident had taken place in a playground rather than a street. Steven's father was a rather preachy politician, and his manner irritated Isabel. *I could bite him myself – the father, that is . . .*

She said the first thing that came to mind. 'Was he provoked?'

She immediately realised that this was the wrong thing to say. Her reaction, though, had been spontaneous – that of any mother confronted with evidence of a child's wrongdoing.

Miss Young looked at her with undisguised disapproval. 'Of course not. It was nothing to do with anything Steven had said or done. And he was very upset – as you may imagine.'

Isabel took a deep breath. She could see Charlie at the end of the corridor, hanging his school bag up on a peg. He was talking to another small boy and ... She gasped. Charlie was leaning forward, as if to bite the other child. But he did not; Isabel had misread the situation. The other boy was showing Charlie something from his bag.

'But that wasn't the only incident of that sort,' Miss Young continued. 'It was the second time he'd done it. The day before, he had bitten Rory on the forearm. Quite a bad bite.'

Isabel's heart lurched. She knew exactly who Rory was: a small boy with red hair and freckles, the son of her dentist. She stared mutely at Miss Young.

'I reprimanded him,' said Miss Young. 'I told him that that sort of behaviour was completely unacceptable.'

'Oh, it is,' said Isabel, struggling to collect her thoughts. 'Biting is ... is ... unacceptable.'

'We can't have it,' said Miss Young, looking at Isabel as if to suggest that she had somehow authorised this outbreak of biting.

'We certainly can't,' Isabel echoed. 'And I assure you, we would never tolerate it at home. We had a little of this sort of thing when he was much smaller, but we'd never put up with it now.'

Miss Young looked as if she found this hard to believe. 'I wouldn't suggest for a moment that you would sanction this sort of thing. But I think you will need to address it.'

'Of course,' said Isabel.

'And its causes,' added Miss Young.

Isabel frowned. Did Miss Young have an idea as to what these causes might be? She decided to ask her directly.

'It's never simple,' the teacher replied. 'Bad behaviour has all sorts of explanations. The child may be worried about something. It may be attention-seeking. It may be caused by some problem at home ... ' She paused. 'There may be tension in the home.'

'There is no tension in our home,' said Isabel. 'None at all. Our home is very ... very *untense*.' Intense, perhaps, but not tense.

Miss Young back-pedalled. 'Of course, of course. I was just saying that these are some of the reasons that one finds from time to time when a child is troublesome.'

'I'll speak to him,' said Isabel. 'I'll make sure it doesn't happen again.'

Miss Young looked relieved. 'I'm sure it won't persist. Often these behavioural hiccups last a week or two and then whatever's worrying the child is sorted out and the bad behaviour stops. I've seen that time and time again.'

Isabel asked the teacher whether she would report any recurrence. 'I take this very seriously,' she said.

'I'm glad to see that,' said Miss Young. 'He's a nice little boy, Charlie. We'd hate to lose him.'

Isabel stared at her, wide-eyed. Would the school react in such a dramatic way to the entirely normal example of playground rough and tumble? For that was what it was, really: children were always scratching or hitting one another – especially little boys. They pushed one another over; they were very physical. Biting was less common, of course, but it was surely just another example of the sort of things that small boys did.

'You wouldn't exclude a child for that?' she asked.

Miss Young closed her eyes briefly, in the way of one about to deliver a sentence. 'In normal circumstances, we wouldn't exclude a violent child ... '

A violent child ... Isabel did not like this description of Charlie. This was her Charlie – the affectionate, amusing little boy who loved A. A. Milne and The Singing Kettle and the other innocent things of childhood. This was not a *violent child*.

'It's not all that serious,' Isabel protested. 'Children have these little spats. It's not a sign of anything more worrying.'

Miss Young looked at her watch. 'I really must dash. We're doing a nature ramble later today.' She sighed. 'Taking twenty-four five-year-olds to Craiglockhart Hill is not exactly easy.'

'I understand,' said Isabel. She did: because now she thought of what might happen with twenty-four small children wandering around in the undergrowth on Craiglockhart Hill – what opportunities there would be for mayhem, for atavistic deeds ... It would be, she thought, *Lord of the Flies* all over again.

Isabel stopped her reverie. 'I shall try to get to the bottom of this ... this bad behaviour, but I want to avoid making too much of a fuss. I'm sure the psychologists would agree that we shouldn't make too much of it.' She paused. 'But I will speak to him – I promise you.'

Miss Young gave her a slightly disapproving look – as if she were registering the promise of one whose word could not be trusted. 'Well then,' she said, and glanced at her watch again.

It occurred to Isabel that she had said nothing about the victims of Charlie's biting spree. 'You said that the bite he gave Rory was a bad one. Did it break the skin?' She really would have to express some regret if there had been actual injury. And of course she felt that regret; it was just that she had not yet had the opportunity to say so.

Miss Young hesitated, and that made Isabel hope for a

moment that the teacher had been exaggerating. The bite, perhaps, was no more than a nip.

'There was no bleeding,' said Miss Young at last. 'Or none by the time it came to my attention.'

Isabel was relieved. 'I'm glad to hear that,' she said.

'But there were very clear tooth marks. There was no doubt that Rory had been bitten.'

Isabel thought that Miss Young was now looking slightly uncomfortable, and she saw the straw at which she might now clutch. 'Are you sure it was Charlie?'

'Oh,' said Miss Young, 'I'm pretty sure it was.'

Isabel took a deep breath. There was something disquieting about arguing with a teacher – it was as if one were answering back in some way, as if one were challenging authority. This was *Miss* Young – not Jeanie Young, or whatever she was called. One might easily dispute the conclusion of a Jeanie Young, but not so readily the conclusion of a *Miss* Young.

'You didn't see it? Not directly?'

Miss Young began to look shifty. *Charlie is being blamed on the basis of inadequate evidence*, Isabel thought. And why? Because he might have subsequently bitten somebody – but even then, what was the evidence for that? Had that bite been witnessed?

'I didn't see the incident myself,' said Miss Young. 'Rory came up to me and said that somebody had bitten him. He showed me the bite. He was in tears, poor child.'

'And then?' asked Isabel. 'What happened then?'

The nature of their conversation had now changed. Isabel was now the interrogator, almost the complainant.

Miss Young was elusive. 'I asked him who did it, and he pointed at Charlie.'

'Did he say anything?' Isabel pressed. 'Did he actually say it was Charlie?'

She wanted to ask whether there had been other children milling around. Had Rory's accusing finger been pointed unambiguously at Charlie, or only in his general direction? That was important, she felt. It was not as if there had been an identity parade, with the children standing in a line, numbers hung about their necks.

'I can't recall,' said Miss Young, 'He was tearful, you have to remember. When they're crying it's hard to make sense of the words sometimes.'

Isabel thought: children of that age have a questionable grasp of the truth. They invent. A false accusation is nothing to a five-year-old. She wanted to say something to that effect, but now Miss Young was reasserting her control. 'I really must get on,' she said. 'Please have a word with him – as you agreed to do.'

Isabel nodded. She would be co-operative – but firm. Miss Young was not going to push her around. There was such a thing as natural justice – and due process. You do *not* go around leaping to conclusions, Miss Young, thought Isabel. You do not.

'I shall,' she said, keeping her voice level. 'I shall try to find out whether he really did bite Rory. And if he did, then I shall certainly do what I can.'

Miss Young's eyes narrowed. 'He bit him,' she said. 'I think you can be sure of that.'

They parted. Miss Young went off, with only a slight glance behind her, to her battle station in the classroom. Isabel turned and walked away from the entrance to the Primary One block – almost directly into her dentist, Rory's father, who was holding the hand of his young son, ready to say goodbye to him.

The dentist looked at her. Isabel blushed. Dentists know, she thought, what it is to be bitten.

But there was no sign of animosity – no flaunting of historical wrong.

'What a gorgeous morning,' said the dentist cheerfully. 'What a pity we have to work.'

She thought of the work that lay ahead of him. The mouths. The saliva. The whine of the high-speed drill. She glanced at Rory, who was looking up at her, smiling. This was not the look of reproach that a child might direct at the mother of an assailant.

She decided to take the bull by the horns. 'I hear there may have been an issue,' she whispered to the dentist.

He looked surprised. 'What sort of issue?'

Isabel nodded towards the entrance to the classroom, where the figure of Miss Young could be seen, surrounded by a small knot of active children.

'Miss Young tells me that Charlie may have bitten Rory.'

The dentist's air of surprise intensified. 'Charlie? Bitten Rory?' He bent down to speak to his son. 'What's all this about a bite, Rory? Did your friend Charlie bite you?'

Rory's eyes widened. He shook his head vigorously.

Cleared, thought Isabel.

'I don't think so,' said the dentist. 'She must have got the wrong end of the stick.' He paused. 'And they're always getting into little scraps, these boys. It makes one wish one had girls. Less physical violence.'

Isabel laughed – half with relief, half at the dentist's comment. A bell sounded, to mark the beginning of the school day. 'I must dash,' she said.

'So must we all,' said the dentist, as Rory tugged at his hand.

Isabel began to walk back towards the school gate. This was a row about nothing. Rory may have been bitten, or he may not. What Miss Young had thought were teeth marks could have been something else altogether – a minor injury inflicted by somebody else: there were twenty-four children in the class, and therefore twenty-three potential suspects. There was, of course, still the question of the bite received by Steven, but the surrounding circumstances of that assault had not been made clear. If there had been a false accusation in one case, then it was perfectly possible that there had been another.

And yet, she thought, and yet Charlie did have a record when it came to biting – an old record, expunged, she had thought, but ... It may be a mother's instinct to defend her child, and it may be easy simply to ignore this whole matter, but what her lawyer friends would call a *prima facie* case had been raised against Charlie and she owed it to Miss Young to do something about it, even if the teacher had been too quick to assume Charlie's guilt. She would speak to him about the importance of not biting people. He was an attentive child, and when she addressed him seriously, he tended to take even the gentlest of criticism to heart. Jamie, no doubt, would underline her message with a few words of his own, and the whole thing would blow over, as something as petty as this should do.

The day, she thought, was improving. She would go back and tackle some editing, which, after all, she was meant to be doing. At noon, though, it being Friday, she would go down to The Chaumer for lunch, where she hoped she might be able to engineer a coincidental meeting with Jamie's delinquent conductor and his lover. She found herself looking forward to that. Sorting out other people's problems could be difficult; it could be time-consuming and distracting. It could even be dangerous. But heaven preserve us, she said to herself, from a life without danger.

9

The Chaumer, a coffee house-cum-bistro described in a restaurant guide as a reassuring pinnacle of old-fashioned good taste, was at the west end of Queen Street, a lengthy thoroughfare lined on its southern side with well-behaved Georgian buildings. The architecture was typical of the Edinburgh New Town – regular and harmonious, the embodiment in stone of the ideal of order. Doors might be painted different colours, but were in their proportions and effect much the same as one another, being distinguished only by their furniture of brass handles and occasional Roman numerals. Through windows neatly divided by astragals, the rooms looked out over formal gardens to the long sweep of Heriot Row, one of the city's most expensive addresses, and beyond that, on the other side of the Firth of Forth, to the hills of Fife, modest, attenuated blue in this northern light.

The Chaumer was owned by the business next door, a traditional outfitter. While The Chaumer served coffee and light meals, the shop next door sold Irish country boots, Scottish scarves and Harris Tweed jackets. Isabel's friend, Vixy, who ran both shops with her business partner, Daniel, lived for wool in all its incarnations: for tweeds and tartans, for kilts and Fair Isle sweaters, and for eccentric shooting hose. She and Isabel shared a taste for muted shades – browns and russets and the natural dyes that produced them, and for the more obscure tartans associated with the minor Scottish clans. The daily running of the restaurant side of the business was handled by a young woman called Claire, whom Isabel knew slightly through Cat. Claire and Cat had been on a knife-skills course together at the Edinburgh New Town Cookery School – 'It sounds like a martial art,' Cat had said. 'But it's actually about filleting fish and chopping up onions.' Claire was petite, in her late twenties, and came from Skye. She spoke softly, and there was in her voice a trace of an accent that was becoming increasingly rare – the West Highland lilt. Movements of people and the baneful effect of electronic communications had eroded that way of speaking, but it could still be heard now and then, like a faint signal in the ether, a reminder of a gentler time. Claire's manner, too, Isabel found instantly appealing. Jamie would have described her as *simpatica*, a word that Isabel thought precisely right in this case. Claire was exactly that – *simpatica*.

That day, as Isabel came through The Chaumer's door, Claire was in the kitchen at the back, unpacking a large cardboard box in which the weekly supply of coffee had been delivered. Claire looked up and waved. Leaving the chef, to whom she was talking, she came over to greet her friend.

'You should have told me you were coming,' she said reproachfully. 'What if I'd been out?'

She invited Isabel to sit down. 'Fortunately, we've got a free table. Are you going to have lunch – or just a coffee?'

'I'll have lunch,' said Isabel. And then, 'Could I persuade you to join me?'

Claire hesitated before accepting. 'I should be in the kitchen.'

'Don't feel under any pressure,' Isabel reassured her. 'I have plenty to think about if I'm to lunch alone.'

'No,' said Claire. 'I'm due a break, and I'd love to.' She signalled to the waiter, a young man with a thin moustache. He brought the menu across and left it on the table. As he went back into the kitchen, Claire leaned forward and whispered to Isabel, 'That's Freddie. He's a student, but he manages ten hours a week here. He's very reliable.'

'That's good. Students can have difficulty with timekeeping.'

Claire rolled her eyes. '*People* can have difficulty with timekeeping.

'He's rather sweet,' she went on. 'I'm sure they could use him to model some of the clothes for our catalogue if he didn't have that moustache.' She made a face. 'It's not *convincing* enough. It's an ... an *attempted* moustache.'

Isabel smiled. 'He must have it for a reason.'

'I think he imagines it makes him more interesting,' said Claire. 'Young men sometimes feel that people don't find them interesting enough. They like the androgynous look these days. They'd like to be like us women – but with the possible addition of a moustache.'

The waiter returned with a bottle of water and they placed their order. Claire enquired after Jamie, and Isabel told her about the Wagner rehearsal in Glasgow. Then she mentioned the ensemble with whom Jamie was playing in Edinburgh. Claire listened for a few moments before interrupting. 'Oh, he comes in here. Their conductor. Larry something-or-other. A tall man.'

'That's him,' said Isabel. 'Jamie just refers to him as

Laurence. He doesn't like being called Larry, apparently.' She paused. She was wondering whether to tell Claire why she was interested in Laurence. She decided not to: she had heard from Jamie that Laurence was having an affair, but he was the only source. Orchestras were gossipy places, and it was possible that Jamie was quite innocently relaying something that was simply untrue. She opted for an innocent question. 'Do you know him?'

Claire shrugged. 'A bit. He has lunch sometimes on Fridays. He'll probably be in today.' She gave Isabel a conspiratorial glance. 'He has friends, you see. Lady friends.'

Isabel raised an eyebrow. 'In the plural?'

Claire nodded. 'Yes. I've seen him with . . . oh, three or four different women.'

'They can't all be girlfriends,' said Isabel. 'Close girl-friends, I mean.'

'Lovers? You'd think not,' said Claire. 'And yet, it does rather seem like it when you see them together. He sits over there, by the window. People always like the same table, you know. He sits there and you see some young woman staring into his eyes. Starstruck would be the word to describe it, I'd say.'

'Simply because he's a conductor?'

Claire seemed to weigh her answer. 'Perhaps. Maybe. Who knows what goes through people's minds when it comes to being attracted to somebody? It's a mystery to me.'

Isabel knew what she meant. Sometimes it was obvious what attracted one person to another. A face could launch a thousand ships . . . Even just one would be enough for most. 'Looks?' she said. 'Just that – nothing more complicated. Looks.'

Claire was not too sure. 'Is it as simple as that? We've got this guy who comes in here – you should see him. Film-star handsome. Fabulous hair. And his eyes . . . See the sky out there? That colour. But he makes me shudder – inside, that is. I'm careful not to shudder when I'm talking to people I can't stand.'

Isabel laughed. 'You're the model of tact, Claire.'

Claire inclined her head in mock acceptance of the compliment. 'Thank you. But there's something about this guy that I just can't bear. I suppose it's his attitude.'

'Is he pleased with himself? Is that it?'

Claire nodded vigorously. 'That's it. That's just what it is. He's not only pleased with himself, he's delighted. Thrilled, even.' Her tone was slightly waspish.

After they had examined the menu and placed their order, the waiter returned a few minutes later with two bowls of soup. 'Soup,' he announced, placing the bowls before them.

'Thank you, Freddie,' said Claire.

'Yup,' said Freddie as he left them.

Claire watched him retreat. 'So sweet,' she mused. 'But he seems to have so few words. He says "soup" from time to time, as we've just heard, and I've heard him say "coffee" and "olives", but not much else.' She thought for a moment. 'Actually, he came in to work yesterday and said "Thursday" – completely unprovoked. I wasn't too sure what to make of it. It was, indeed, Thursday, but was it a special Thursday? I have no idea. It might have been ... '

'An adumbration,' Isabel suggested.

Claire frowned. 'Possibly,' she said. And then, as an afterthought, 'Whatever that means.'

'It's a favourite word of mine,' said Isabel. 'Not that I ever get the chance to use it. It's so cumbersome – the sort of word one carries around just in case one will get the chance to dust it down and put it in a sentence.'

'I still don't know what it means,' Claire complained.

128

'I only knew it because I went off to the dictionary to look it up. It's not a word one learns at one's mother's knee.'

'No,' Claire agreed. 'Like *pejorative*. I love that word. Using it is almost cathartic.'

'Like *cathartic* itself. Saying *cathartic* has a . . . well, a cathartic effect.'

'But *adumbration*?' asked Claire.

'It's a vague statement about the implications of something or other. It could also be a prediction of a very general sort.'

'Such as "there's going to be trouble"?'

'Exactly. That's an adumbration.'

'So, *Thursday* might mean – things that are known to happen on Thursdays are going to happen today. Is that it?'

'Yes,' said Isabel. 'But heaven knows what those things are.'

They both laughed. Isabel, though, was thinking about something she had read a short while ago. In a second-hand bookstore in the West Port, she had picked up a volume of psychoanalytical essays. The book, entitled *The World of Emotions*, was over forty years old, and had travelled. It had been published in New York, and it bore on the title page the name and address of a previous owner, a Dr Lionel Katz MD, with an address in Brooklyn. Here and there in the text, Dr Katz had made an annotation in pencil, sometimes with a reference to a journal article somewhere, sometimes with an exclamation mark, and occasionally with the name of what Isabel imagined was one of his patients. On impulse, she had bought the book and on returning home had immersed herself in it. She found herself thinking of Dr Katz, and how it was that the book had found its way across the Atlantic to end up on a dusty lower shelf in a Scottish bookshop. And she wondered about Dr Katz, whom she felt she would like, on the slender basis of his pencilled notes. She could almost see him, in his slightly dishevelled suit, with his horn-rimmed spectacles and bow tie, sitting in his office, with its inevitable couch, and his bookcases groaning under the weight of the psychoanalytical journals. Dr Katz would be dead now, she decided, because she imagined that when he bought the book he was already in his fifties, if not even older. *The World of Emotions* had been published in 1977 – a more innocent time, she thought, when people still believed that life would get steadily better. And it still might, she decided, if only we learned how to co-operate with one another.

One of the essays in the book was on smugness, and she had chosen to read this before she progressed to arrogance, pouting, bitterness, or pathological jealousy. Now she told Claire about how her comments had reminded her of what she had read, adding, 'Smugness is very odd, you know.'

Claire looked puzzled. 'Really? It's just . . . what is it? Being really pleased with oneself.'

'It's more than that,' said Isabel. 'It entails having a certain attitude to the world. The smug are indifferent to what other people think of them. They don't really care what you think because they're indifferent to your approbation or disapproval. Everything about themselves is absolutely perfect and what *you* think about that state of affairs is neither here nor there.'

Claire tackled her soup. 'We mustn't let this get cold while we sit here talking about smugness.'

'But what's particularly interesting,' Isabel continued, 'is the different sort of reactions that smugness triggers in others. If you're insecure, if you're uncertain about your own worth, then seeing smugness can drive you up the wall.'

Claire lowered her gaze. Isabel did not notice.

'That's what I read,' Isabel continued. 'It gave examples of patients who became aroused to the point of violence when

130

confronted with a smug person. Apparently, people who are a bit fragile themselves want nothing more than to slap the smug in the face – they really do. A smug face, apparently, is like a red rag to a bull to insecure people.'

Isabel suddenly became aware that Claire was staring at her. 'But that's me,' Claire said quietly. 'That's how I feel. I find myself wanting to punch our good-looking friend.' She looked embarrassed, and lowered her voice. 'Not that I ever would.'

'No,' said Isabel. 'I don't see that happening.'

'But what you said suggests that I'm insecure,' said Claire. 'Am I, do you think?'

Isabel caught her breath. She had offended her friend. She should have thought before she spoke. 'Of course not,' she said quickly. 'Those were extreme cases. What you describe is just normal irritation. It's what we all feel.'

'No,' said Claire. 'It's not quite the same thing. He sends my blood pressure through the roof. He makes me livid. The mere sight of him does that.'

Isabel tried to make light of it. 'Oh, I'm sure you're exaggerating.'

Claire pursed her lips before replying. 'I'm not. I should know how I feel.'

Isabel looked at her soup. She could say something about that. A comment about soup could defuse the situation.

'This soup is delicious,' she said. 'I love . . . ' She suddenly realised she did not know what was in the soup. It was tasty enough, but it could have been anything, and when she had glanced at the menu it had simply said 'Soup of the Day'. So she trailed off, rather lamely, 'I love soup.'

Claire had finished hers, and now she looked at her watch. 'I really should get back to the kitchen,' she said.

Isabel assured her that she would be happy to have coffee

131

by herself, and Claire rose to leave the table. She was still offended, Isabel thought. Isabel had effectively accused her of being insecure, and she had not taken it well. Isabel thought about that, and might have devised some means of making up for her tactlessness, but now the door onto the street had opened and a tall man was making his way to a table near the window. There was a woman with him – a younger woman who was wearing a light green linen blouse and white skirt. She had a sweater tied loosely around her waist – a precaution, Isabel thought, against unexpected changes in temperature at this end of the summer.

To Isabel's relief, the table the couple chose was within earshot.

'You get caught out in September, Laurence,' the young woman was saying. 'It's getting cooler in the evenings now – have you noticed?'

Laurence muttered something that Isabel did not hear. But she heard him call the young woman Annette. Or, thought Isabel, did he say 'Athene'? No, she was sure it was Annette.

'It's not a big menu,' Laurence now said. 'Which is a good thing, in my view. A few things, well chosen, are better than a massive choice.'

'Always,' said Annette.

Then Laurence said, 'Did you go to Glasgow?'

'Yes,' she replied. 'I had to go over there to stand in for somebody – just for a couple of rehearsals. The person's back now. She was having an operation. A cyst – a big one, apparently. A tennis ball, she said.'

'Oh,' said Laurence.

'Scottish Opera. The *Meistersingers*. Enjoyable enough.'

Laurence was examining the menu. 'A couple of our people are playing in it. Our bassoonist, for one.'

Isabel had brought a book with her. Now she opened it, and stared at the page.

'Oh, him,' said Annette. 'The dishy one.'

The printed page swam before Isabel's eyes.

'Yes. Jamie.'

'He's gorgeous,' said Annette. 'I find it hard to keep my eyes off him. I saw him at the Queen's Hall a few weeks ago. I was hoping to chat to him ...'

'Do you have a preferred chat-up line?' asked Laurence.

'I thought I might say, "Do you play here often?" Or maybe, "I've always loved the bassoon." Which is true, actually – I do love the bassoon.'

Laurence laughed. 'The old lines are always the best.' Then he added reproachfully, 'Flirt.'

'I think he noticed me,' said Annette.

'Of course he would,' said Laurence. 'People like him have an eye for girls like you.'

'I'll let that pass,' said Annette. She began to scrutinise the menu. 'There's a pie. Do you see there's a pie? I think I'm going to have a pie – it's ages since I had one.'

Annette now glanced across the table, directly at Isabel. For a moment their eyes met, before they both looked away again. It was an accidental meeting – the sort of thing that happens in a restaurant when people may briefly speculate about their fellow diners.

Isabel tried to concentrate on the book she had opened. It was André Comte-Sponville's *A Short Treatise on the Great Virtues*. She had opened the book at the beginning of the chapter on prudence. A small speck of butter, detritus from the bread that had accompanied her soup, had landed on a page of the book to produce a tiny, oily stain, like a minor island on a map. Isabel tried to flick it off, but only made it worse

133

and smudged it further. She looked up in annoyance, to see Annette whispering something to Laurence while she was, once again, looking at Isabel.

She returned to the virtues, struggling to concentrate, while at the same time listening to the conversation at the other table. I am an eavesdropper, she said to herself. I am a common eavesdropper. She closed the book and stood up. Going to the back of the room, she paid her bill. Claire came up to her to say goodbye.

'I was very tactless,' said Isabel. 'I'm very sorry if I offended you.'

Claire looked at her in astonishment. 'What are you talking about?' she asked.

'What I said about smugness and people who are offended by smug people.'

Claire laughed. 'Oh, that? No, you're absolutely right. I *am* insecure, I think, but I don't really mind. We're all a bit that way, aren't we?'

Isabel's relief showed. 'Of course we are. I worry about all sorts of things.'

'It's all to do with having an elder sister,' Claire went on. 'Fiona attracted more attention than I did.' She paused. 'But I really don't mind. She and I get on very well now.'

'I'm glad.'

Isabel became aware that Freddie was watching them. 'Thank you,' she said to him. 'I enjoyed that soup.'

He nodded. 'Squash.'

So that was what it was, thought Isabel. But there had been something else. Ham, perhaps?

Claire and Isabel exchanged glances before Isabel left, walking past Laurence's table as she made her way to the door. The things at which we should not look have a particular magnetic field, but she managed to keep her eyes averted She heard, though, very clearly, what was being said at the table.

'You have to commit, Laurence. You have to.'

He sighed – audibly – and then replied, 'All right, all right, all right.'

10

Jamie's rehearsal in Glasgow that morning had finished by eleven, enabling him, after a quick dash to Queen Street Station, to be back in Edinburgh by twelve-thirty. He liked to get off the train at Haymarket Station, in the west of the city, and then walk home partly along the canal towpath. August had been unusually warm, and now, even in the first week of September, people were still in shirt-sleeves and shorts, one or two of them sunbathing on the canal-side, briefly indifferent to the fading of summer. The inhabitants of northern cities are not slow to snatch at such warmth as comes their way, unselfconsciously exposing to the sun – as they did now – pallid limbs and faces. Jamie walked past some of these sun-worshippers and reflected on the fact that another summer had gone past without the trip to Greece that he and Isabel had talked about, and even begun to plan. A musician friend had a house on a small Ionian island, and had offered to let them have the use of it, but the dates had not worked out. Isabel had fallen behind with work on a forthcoming special issue of the *Review,* and he had rashly accepted a short touring commitment — three days in Aberdeen and Inverness — that came at just the wrong time. Had they been better organised, he could be doing what these people were doing — sitting in the sun — but on a beach, or the terrace of a house in an olive grove, or somewhere rather more suitable than the edge of a Scottish canal. But that was not to be, and he began to think, instead, of how he was going to deal with the matter that he had promised Isabel he would look into. That was another rash promise, he thought, and he should not have made it. How could he be expected to make the remotest difference to this rather petty family quarrel in which Isabel had somehow become involved? It was not her business, and neither should it be his. Even the question of the orchestral appointment was, arguably, nothing to do with him. He was a member of the orchestra, not one of its managers. If Laurence was acting corruptly — or planning to do so — then that should be a matter for the board, not for rank-and-file players like him, and certainly not for Isabel.

By the time he reached the house, he was in a state of confusion. He had decided, as he crossed the canal bridge at Harrison Gardens, that he would speak to Isabel as soon as she got back from lunch and tell her that he was proposing not to interfere in the Douglas family feud, and that it would be better, all round, if she kept out of orchestral affairs. He had already rehearsed the lines he would use to drive that point home: *The world is full of injustices we can't realistically do anything about. All we have to do is try to prevent ourselves acting unjustly — that's all. If everybody did that, then injustice and unfairness would wither away.* The first point was an important one: he had been married to a philosopher long enough to know about Kant's Categorical Imperative, that we should act as if our actions were to be performed by all. He had heard Isabel talking about it, and surely what he was now suggesting was perfectly in accord with what Kant recommended. And yet, even as he thought it, he realised that if everybody restricted themselves in that way, then all sorts of wrongs would go unaddressed. The world, he realised, needed people who took it upon themselves to intervene. The world needed people like Isabel.

His resolve faltered as he made his way past the tennis club. He would have to do something. He would not try to stop her dealing with Laurence. In fact, it would serve Laurence right to be exposed for the cheat that he was. Was he a cheat? Or was there some other term for one who abused their office? Did it matter all that much what word one applied? There were plenty of colourful expressions, after all, that would do the work of more sophisticated moral terminology. *Sleazebag* – that was a good one, and rather suited the conductor. Then there was *creep*, which had a good ring to it and was almost onomatopoeic . . . Jamie felt slightly better, and now he was at the front door, key in hand, and the door opened before him, as if it had anticipated him.

Grace stood on the threshold.

'I saw you from the sitting-room window,' she said. 'I was dusting. You should see the dust that's accumulated above the pelmet.'

She gave Jamie a slightly reproachful look, as if he was responsible for the build-up. Then she asked, 'Have you had any lunch?'

Jamie replied that he had eaten an apple on the train. He would need something else.

'I was about to make myself a sandwich,' Grace said. 'I could make one for you. Ham? Or cheese?'

He followed her into the kitchen and sat down at the table

while she prepared the sandwiches. He watched her: reliable, salt of-the-earth Grace, who played such an important part in their lives, just as she had done in the life of Isabel's father. Grace had come with the house, so to speak; she had kept it for years and it was impossible to think of it without her. She was the classic family retainer, and yet that was a concept with which Jamie had never been entirely comfortable It seemed somehow wrong to him that one person should devote her whole life to looking after another, even if it was a role that was freely chosen. He was not sure why it should be wrong, although it seemed to him that it might be something to do with the inherent inequality of the arrangement: a servant was always beholden to the employer, and however much the employer treated the servant as an equal, he or she simply was not. Equals can dispense with one another if they wish; equals cannot tell the other what to do; equals can disagree and answer back with impunity.

Of course, Jamie understood that whatever his misgivings about Grace's situation might be, it would be inconceivable – and wrong – for Isabel no longer to employ Grace. And if Isabel were to dispense with Grace's services – out of embarrassment at having a housekeeper when nobody they knew had one, or would ever think of having one – what would that achieve? Grace would be devastated. She felt entitled to this job, and she did it well. The house was run smoothly and efficiently, giving Isabel time to fulfil her editorial role. That had a knock-on beneficial effect that spread out its ripples across the world of academic philosophy. If Isabel were to give up the *Review*, it would disappear. It was Isabel who paid the bills, using the funds she had inherited from her mother's side of the family, earned by the company that she rarely spoke about but that ultimately guaranteed everything – not just the *Review*, with all its expenses, but also the extensive network of causes that Isabel supported. There were the obvious arts bodies – the ballet, the opera, the galleries – where Isabel's name could be seen among those of other supporters in the printed programmes at events, but Jamie knew there were scores of less obvious causes that she supported. And they knew it too, which meant that the requests kept coming, and Isabel, being unable to say no, or at least finding it immensely difficult to do so, usually wrote a cheque. Jamie was proud of that. He had often told her that she should be careful not to spread herself too thinly, that she could not help absolutely everybody who came to her with a request to do something or the other, but he knew that his counsel would, at the end of the day, have little effect. We did what we did. That was a simple way of putting it, but it was nonetheless true. Few people changed; most behaved the way they did because of traits that were deeply engrained. How you look at things, Isabel had once observed, is like hair colour. Jamie had wondered what she meant, because she'd offered no further explanation, but on thinking about it, he realised that her remark was quite apposite. The colour of our hair was nothing to do with us. We might dye it, of course, and the dye may make the hair look different, but the real colour showed itself at the roots.

Grace produced his sandwich with a flourish. 'I've given you ham, cheese, lettuce and a good dollop of mayonnaise,' she said. 'People stint on mayonnaise, but that's so stupid. It really is a pity.'

Jamie looked at the sandwich, with its mayonnaise seeping out of the sides. 'I like a messy sandwich,' he said. 'I like getting physical with them.'

Grace shot him a glance. 'There's a paper napkin to wipe your fingers,' she said. 'There. Over there.'

'I wasn't criticising your sandwich,' Jamie reassured her. Grace had her touchy side, and both Jamie and Isabel had to be careful. But she was reassured now by the relish with which he tackled the sandwich.

'Mayonnaise is good for you,' said Grace as she picked up her own sandwich. 'As is ham, and cheese too.'

Jamie smiled as he wiped at his lips with the napkin. The mayonnaise had dripped onto his fingers, and he discreetly attended to those too. 'Ham's good for you? Are you sure?'

'Yes, it is,' said Grace briskly. 'It's good for us because we like it. Same goes for bacon, which is the same thing, of course.'

Jamie's eyes widened. 'But I thought bacon was actually rather bad for us. Didn't the WHO make a big thing of it a little while ago? Didn't they warn us not to eat processed meats?'

'They did,' said Grace. 'But all I'm saying is that we have to have *some* things we like. If we don't, then we become miserable, and if we're miserable, you know what happens? We become ill. Nobody's going to argue against that, are they?'

Jamie hesitated. 'Yes, but—'

Grace cut him short. 'I listened to something on the radio the other day about our immune system. It was really interesting. This man who was talking was a real expert on the immune system. He was a professor of immunity somewhere. Glasgow, I think. Or Aberdeen. Somewhere.'

'Immunology,' said Jamie. 'A professor of immunology.'

Grace nodded. 'That's what he was. Immunity. And he said that they had evidence now that if you're lonely, then you're more likely to die. He said you had a twenty-five per cent higher chance of dying than people who weren't lonely.'

'Because your immune system is weaker?'

'Yes. That's exactly what he said. He said that if your

141

immune system is not as strong as it might be, then you get all sorts of diseases, and that will shorten your life.'

'What's this got to do with bacon?'

Grace now spoke as if she were explaining something to Charlie. 'It's simple. If you're happy, you feel good, right? If eating things you like makes you feel good, then you're going to want to mix with other people. You'll have lots of friends, you see. And your immune system will be better too. It'll protect you.'

'And mayonnaise?' asked Jamie.

'That's good for you too,' said Grace. 'Not just because it makes you feel better, but because it has all sorts of good things in it. Eggs, for instance. Eggs are good for your eyes. And vitamin D, I think. Maybe not, but I think it may have vitamin D in it and we need to have more vitamin D in Scotland. We don't get enough because we're a northern country. There's much more vitamin D down south.'

'It's to do with sunlight,' said Jamie.

Grace took a bite of her sandwich. 'Sunlight,' she said through a mouthful. 'That's another thing. They say don't go out in the sun because it'll damage your skin, but then if you don't get sunlight you'll not get enough vitamin D.'

'Possibly not,' agreed Jamie.

'And you'll be miserable too,' Grace added. 'We need summer. We need at least a little bit of time when we can feel cheerful. Summer's really good for the immune system.'

Jamie finished his sandwich. He wanted to talk to Grace, but he felt they had had enough of bacon and mayonnaise and the immune system. He stood up. 'I'll make us tea,' he said. 'Would you like a cup?'

Grace nodded, and Jamie moved to the sink to fill the kettle. 'There's something I want to talk to you about,' he said.

Grace smiled encouragingly. 'Then we'll need the tea.'

'Yes,' said Jamie. 'It'll help.'

Grace waited.

'I don't know what to do,' Jamie began.

'Do about what?'

Jamie sighed. 'You know how Isabel gets involved in things? In other people's problems?'

Grace laughed. 'I certainly do.'

'I keep asking her not to,' Jamie said. 'Or, at least, I used to. I've rather given up recently, and left her to get on with it.' He paused. 'Of course, I'm secretly rather proud of what she does. At least she tries to help. I don't do very much.'

Grace looked thoughtful. 'I admire her too,' she said. 'I know some of the things she's done.'

Jamie gave Grace an appreciative look. 'It's just that ...' He shrugged. 'Well, she can't say no to anybody. And people sense that, I think. They say to themselves, "Here's somebody who can help," and nine times out of ten they're right: she can help, and she does.'

'Which is just as well,' said Grace.

'Yes.'

She gave him a searching look. 'But now? Has she bitten off more than she can chew?'

Jamie shook his head. 'No, I have.'

He explained what had happened. He told her that he had offered to help Isabel without thinking about it, and now that he had given the matter a bit more thought, he had come to the conclusion that it was not the sort of situation where an outsider could do very much. He told her about the Douglas parents and their strained relationship with their son, Richard. 'I don't even know where to begin,' he concluded. 'Should I just go and see this person ... Richard? He works in that wine shop at Holy Corner. What do I do? Do I go and tell him to talk to his father? I think that sounds ridiculous. You can't just go up to somebody like that and start talking to them about family disagreements.'

Grace agreed that you could not. 'And yet,' she pointed out, 'that's exactly the sort of thing Isabel does.'

'I know,' said Jamie. 'I've seen her do it time and time again.'

'Often successfully,' added Grace.

Jamie had to admit that this was true. 'She gets away with it,' he said.

Grace was looking at him intently, as if trying to work out what he was really feeling. 'What do you want me to say?' she asked.

Her question took him by surprise. He had not been expecting any concrete advice from Grace; he wanted her, he supposed, to agree that there was not much, if anything, he could do.

He didn't answer, but merely shrugged. Grace watched him. Then she said, 'Would you like me to do something?'

He had not thought of that, and he answered automatically, 'Yes.' Then added, 'But no, I don't want to burden you with something that's definitely not your business, or mine – or even Isabel's, for that matter.'

Grace smiled. 'It wouldn't be a burden.'

'You mean—'

She cut him short. 'I mean that I could deal with this in my way.'

He was curious. 'And what way is that?'

Grace was finishing her sandwich, and Jamie waited for her reply.

'I have ways of finding out things,' she said.

He stared at her. *I have ways of finding out things*. That had a strange, almost ominous ring to it. He knew that Grace was interested in the paranormal. She was a regular participant at séances and often reported on the latest medium to address her parapsychology group. Was this what she was now suggesting?

She might have guessed his thought. 'No, I don't mean that.'

Jamie grinned. 'No ouija boards or spirit writing?'

'No.' She became serious. 'You shouldn't take those things lightly.'

'I don't,' he assured her. And then, with a certain flippancy, 'I wouldn't dare.'

Grace's eyes narrowed, but she did not say anything. 'What you may not know,' she said, 'is that those of us who work in people's houses have a network.'

Jamie waited.

'And that network,' Grace continued, a note of satisfaction, almost pride, in her voice, 'reaches into most corners of Edinburgh. So, if I want to know what's happening in, say, Murrayfield, or Trinity – or anywhere, really – I have only to ask a few questions.'

'And then you find out?'

'Yes, and then I find out.'

Jamie thought for a moment. 'Okay,' he said. He mentioned a street at random. 'India Street. What's going on in India Street?'

India Street was in the Georgian New Town, a wide street lined on each side with elegant stone tenements. It was a fashionable address – not as sought after, perhaps, as Heriot Row round the corner, or Moray Place, but nonetheless the sort of street in which those with social aspirations might like to live.

Grace did not reply immediately. Then she said, with a flicker of a smile, 'You mean you haven't heard?'

Jamie was not sure whether she was joking. He scrutinised her expression, but it was hard to tell. He shook his head. 'I never hear these things,' he said. That was true; his circle of friends – musicians for the most part – exchanged musical gossip, but that was specialised and not the sort of news that interested others.

'I don't like to trade tittle-tattle,' said Grace.

He was not having that. 'But we all do that. Even . . . even the Pope likes a good story.'

Jamie wondered whether that was true; perhaps it was. The Pope, he thought, or at least the current holder of that office, seemed to have a relaxed manner. And there was a human twinkle in his eye that suggested he would not mind a bit of Vatican gossip – nothing hurtful, of course, nothing mean, but a few amusing details of some remark made by a hapless archbishop or cardinal – that sort of thing.

'There's a difference,' insisted Grace. 'Idle gossip is idle gossip. Facts are another thing altogether.'

'If you say so,' said Jamie. He wanted to find out about India Street, and was less interested in pursuing moral distinctions. Grace must have picked that up from Isabel, who had been splitting philosophical hairs for as long as he had known her. So he said, 'What about India Street?'

Grace drew a deep breath, as if settling in for the long haul. 'There are two couples who live on opposite sides of the street. They've been there for some time, and of course everybody knows them because, well, everybody knows one another in Edinburgh, don't they?'

Jamie agreed. The city's intimacy was one of its greatest merits, although sometimes, of course, it led to difficulties. You had to assume, Isabel once said, that the person *to* whom you're talking is the cousin of the person *about* whom you're talking. A failure to make this assumption could lead to awkward moments.

Grace continued her story. 'Well, these two couples know one another, but not particularly well. Then one of the men started to have an affair with the wife of the other. That sort of thing happens, of course, but what makes this unusual is that the husband of the wife who's having an affair started having an affair with the wife of the man who's having an affair with *his* wife.'

Jamie's eyes widened.

'And neither husband knows what his wife is doing, and neither wife knows what her husband is doing. What do you think of that?'

Jamie looked confused. 'In India Street?' was all he could think of to say.

'Yes, in India Street. It looks so respectable, doesn't it?'

Then he thought: if none of the people involved knew the full story, then how did Grace? He raised this question, politely, concerned that Grace might take offence at being doubted, but she was unfazed.

'That's my point,' she said. 'I happen to know the person who cleans for one of those couples. And she knows the person who cleans for the people over the road. Between them, they have most of the street covered.'

Jamie laughed. He should have guessed. 'I suppose people in your position see everything.'

'We do,' said Grace. 'We see all the details. We don't miss much. We take note ... ' She broke off. Her admission was already too great. 'Of course, I don't snoop,' she said.

'Of course not,' said Jamie hurriedly. But he thought: Grace knows all about us. Yet that, he told himself, was not too discomforting a thought. He and Isabel had no dark secrets, as far as he knew. No, he could be more categorical than that: they definitely had nothing to hide.

'And I respect the principle of confidentiality,' Grace continued. 'I would never reveal what goes on in this house.'

'No,' said Jamie, and then added, 'Not that anything goes on, anyway.'

'No,' said Grace – a little regretfully, thought Jamie.

He reverted to the subject in hand. 'Are you saying that you'd use your network of . . . ' He was about to say 'spies', but stopped himself in time, and said, instead, 'contacts to find out about Richard and his friend, and then . . . '

'Do something about it?' Grace supplied.

'I don't think there's much that can be done,' said Jamie. 'But I suppose they would like to find out what's going on. I gather that they would like to know a bit more about what they're up against.'

Grace became matter-of-fact. 'That's reasonable enough. If you knew that there was somebody disrupting your family – splitting it, really – then you'd have a few questions you might like to ask.'

'Yes, I imagine I would.'

Grace made her offer. 'I could see what I can find out.'

He gave her a grateful look. 'Thank you,' he said. And then he said, 'I'll tell Isabel.'

Grace shook her head. 'Not just yet. Let me have a word with some people first. You can tell Isabel later. Besides, she might not approve.'

Jamie hesitated. He did not like the thought of deceiving Isabel, and he mentioned this to Grace. But it seemed as if she had anticipated his misgivings, as she went on to say, 'It's not deceiving. Not telling somebody about something they do not need to know is not deceiving.'

He would have to think about that, Jamie decided. But for the moment he would leave Grace to do things her way, and he would see what came of it. And he did not think that Isabel would have cause to complain about his having involved Grace. After all, she had delegated her role to him, and so she could hardly complain if he, in turn, delegated it to somebody else. Besides, he thought that Grace was rather more likely than he was to achieve something here, with her newly disclosed network of informants. So he simply nodded, thus indicating his assent to the plan. Now he could get back to thinking about the things that he should really be thinking about, which did not include the problems of a politically intolerant son, his prejudiced boyfriend, and an overbearing father. People made a mess of their lives, he thought. They fought with one another, even with members of their own family, because they were not prepared to live and let live. He had no time for that sort of thing. I could *never* be a politician, he thought, because that was the reason they got out of bed in the morning – to argue with other people; to criticise those who did not agree with them; to say unpleasant things about their opponents. Did it have to be like that, or was it just that the wrong sort of politicians had seized the upper hand and had poisoned the wells of our public life? He sighed. Isabel got him involved in this sort of thing and he did not like it. Perhaps he should not have involved Grace, but he had done it now, and he felt only relief. Isabel and Grace were better at this sort of thing than he was – far better, as he was confident events would in due course demonstrate.

11

That evening Grace went home to her flat in Stockbridge and prepared herself a dinner of fried cod's roe accompanied by salad and mustard potatoes. Jamie had shown her how to make mustard potatoes, which he said went particularly well with fish, and which were very easy to prepare. 'Boil the potatoes, then add butter, chives – if you have them – and a bit of mustard,' he said. 'That's all you need to do. Delicious.'

The potatoes went well with the tinned roe and with the salad, too, over which Grace had sprinkled pine nuts and sliced black olives. A small glass of New Zealand white wine, from a half-case that Isabel had given to her on her last birthday, which she had carefully husbanded since then, completed the meal. Grace was frugal: the pine nuts were an extravagance, but the olives came from a dented can from a special shelf at the supermarket where slightly damaged products were sold at less than half price. 'I have Aberdonian blood in me,' she once explained to Isabel. 'A grandfather on one side, and a grandmother on the other. They knew how to be careful with what little money they had, I can tell you. Have you heard of "tatties and a pass"?'

Isabel had not, and Grace explained: 'In the days when meat was a real treat, the children had to hold back at the table. People thought that the father needed it more than anybody else because he was doing the heavy work. Ploughing. Going down the pits or whatever.'

'And he often was,' said Isabel. 'Though women did more than their fair share of back-breaking work.'

Grace did not disagree. 'True, but that's the way things were in those days. So they gave the children potatoes and they were allowed to pass them over the pot containing the meat. That gave their tatties a whiff of meat. Tatties and a pass, you see. They weren't allowed to dip them into the stew.'

Grace did not apologise for her Aberdonian frugality. Envelopes were reused, the name and address of the original recipient having a label pasted over it and the back flap being rejuvenated with glue made out of flour and water. Grace disapproved of the glue that Isabel bought for the children to use when making paper sculptures. 'Nothing wrong with flour and water,' she said. 'It's much cheaper in the long run.'

Now, with cod's roe, salad and potatoes finished and not a crumb remaining of the oatcake and cheese that constituted the second course, Grace drained the last drops of her half-glass of Marlborough Sounds Sauvignon Blanc. Glancing at her watch, she saw that she had a full half-hour to kill before she made her way up the hill to the Masonic Hall in Thistle Street where her psychic group, the Second Circle of Light, met every other week. Grace had only recently joined the Second Circle of Light, having drifted away from the spiritualist group she had attended for some years. This new group was smaller than her previous one, thus allowing participants more direct access to the invited medium. And the mediums invited to the Second Circle of Light, she thought, were somehow fresher and more innovative, and more likely to come up with communications of interest. At the previous meeting, there had been a frisson of excitement when the medium, who had travelled down to Edinburgh from Inverness for the séance, revealed that Mary, Queen of Scots had been present, although only briefly, and had indicated that she would have something to say about the murder of her secretary, Rizzio, but would keep this disclosure for a subsequent occasion 'when she was less busy'. This had caused a buzz of excited chatter; to make contact with Mary was quite a coup, and her conversation would surely be considerably more interesting than the usual, rather mundane traffic from the other side.

She spent the half-hour before her departure doing her ironing. She did not mind ironing, as it gave her the opportunity to think about the events of the day and plan the week ahead. There was to be a visit to her cousin in Falkirk – probably that Friday – and there would be a lot to discuss on that occasion. They would have to discuss what to do about an aunt of theirs who was needing a bit more care but was unwilling to go into a residential home. The cousin was a school administrator and knew how to make arrangements: she would sort it out, thought Grace, but they would have to tread carefully in view of their aunt's pride.

That did not take long to think about, and Grace was then able to reflect on her lunch with Jamie and the rather unexpected turn that their conversation had taken. It was all Isabel's fault, Grace felt: Isabel was constantly getting mixed up in the affairs of others, and although she seemed to get away with it most of the time, sooner or later she would come unstuck.

The source of the problem, Grace thought, was guilt – Isabel felt guilty because she had money – it was as simple as that. If she didn't have it, then she wouldn't have to justify her existence by creating tasks for herself. If she had an ordinary job and an ordinary house, then she wouldn't have to apologise for her good fortune. She was not lazy; Grace thought, in fact, that Isabel worked rather too hard on occasions. And that *Review* of hers seemed to be a bottomless pit, with all the bills she had to pay and all the prima donna authors she had to placate – those tiresome people who had nothing better to do than write articles about what we should or should not do. They, she noted, didn't do anything most of the time, but they still thought they had the right to lecture the world in general. That awful Professor Lettuce, for instance, in all his pomposity – and that *creepy* Christopher Dove: they gave philosophy a bad name, as far as Grace was concerned. Unlike Aristotle, about whom Isabel occasionally talked, and whom Grace imagined quite clearly, and of whom she was inclined to approve. He would have been a distinguished-looking man, she decided, with a very courteous manner; the sort of man who always got to his feet when somebody entered the room. He would have a slightly distant air, as if he was really somewhere else altogether; Greece, perhaps. She could see herself having tea with Aristotle in Isabel's sitting room, telling him that Isabel would be back from the supermarket shortly and would be so pleased to see that he had dropped in. She thought he would probably prefer Earl Grey tea to their ordinary Assam, but he would never say anything, of course, if you gave him tea that he did not really like. Yes, Aristotle would be easy to entertain – unlike Immanuel Kant, whom Isabel occasionally invoked. Isabel had told her about Kant's scrupulous punctuality, and that had not endeared him to

Grace. 'The citizens of Königsberg could set their watches by him,' Isabel had said. 'He always went off for his walk at precisely the same hour and returned at exactly the same time every day.' He would have been fussy, Grace decided, and also very dull to listen to. She pictured herself being followed round the house by Kant while she tried to make the beds and do the vacuuming. He would drone on and on and it would exhaust her. It would be impossible to be married to Immanuel Kant, she thought, although there may well have been some poor woman who was in that position and who had, no doubt, borne it with fortitude. Aristotle's wife was more difficult to place. She might have been a fairly racy sort, rather too glamorous for somebody like Aristotle, who, being concerned with higher things, would put up with her flirting with the young men in her husband's academy or the man who brought the olive oil round to the house. She might even be the sort of woman whose eye might fall on somebody like Christopher Dove.

Grace shuddered as she thought of Dove, who looked like a fair-haired version of that actor who played Dracula in the old black and white films, whatever his name was. Yes, him: and he might easily have been called Christopher Dove, which she had always felt was a very sinister name. She could not imagine what it would be like to be in the same room as him. She went further and imagined what it would be like to be *married* to either of them – to have Lettuce pontificating over the breakfast table or Christopher Dove slouching about in his pyjamas ... It was a frightening thought. Actually, being married to any man was not something that Grace liked to think about too much. Oh, it was necessary, of course; sex, as one of Grace's friends had once observed, is here to stay. And if it involved the right sort of man, there was something to be said for it. Jamie, for instance . . . but then he was already taken and one should not think about men who were already taken – that was something that Grace's mother had drummed into her before she left home. 'Find out whether a man is taken,' she warned. 'There are plenty of men who pretend they're free, and they aren't. Don't even look at those men, Grace. Just say, "No thank you." And if they persist, tell them that you look forward to meeting their wives. That stops them in their tracks most of the time.'

The pile of ironing was not large, and Grace slowed down, taking particular care with the pleats of a favourite blouse. Her thoughts had drifted, and she now found herself thinking of what had happened that afternoon, when, after her sandwich with Jamie, she had set off to collect Charlie and Magnus from school. Grace usually did the school walk when Isabel had a printer's deadline looming, as was now the case, with only a couple of days remaining before all the copy for the next issue had to be dispatched. She enjoyed the task, as it gave her a chance to see what was going on in the busy purlieus of the school. The two boys also enjoyed seeing her, and would vie with each other for her attention as they regaled her with stories of what had happened in school. The school day, it seemed, was punctuated with incidents of high drama. Alliances were made, and broken; episodes of injustice and unfairness were legion; good behaviour stars were won and lost; and in between all this, the demands of education were occasionally observed.

It was while they were walking back, and about to cross Colinton Road, that Magnus suddenly let out a piercing yell. The two boys had been standing beside her, waiting for the pedestrian crossing light, and for a few moments Grace's attention had been distracted. There had been a steady stream

155

of traffic, and she was looking to see whether a large delivery van, which had been lumbering down the road, was going to stop for the signal. It was at this point that Magnus's protest was raised.

Grace looked down sharply. Magnus had raised his arms and was covering his eyes, as if in pain. Charlie, standing beside him, was looking fixedly ahead, as if indifferent to the disturbance beside him.

'Magnus!' exclaimed Grace. 'What's wrong?'

Magnus lowered his hands. His eyes were streaming with tears.

For a moment or two, Grace imagined that he had been stung by something. There were bees about – she had seen one a few minutes earlier – and it may have alighted on him. Now she bent down to comfort him. Charlie moved from foot to foot, waiting impatiently.

'Charlie bit me,' Magnus wailed, waving his right hand, the evidence, in front of Grace.

Grace examined the hand. One of the fingers looked a bit red, but the skin was unbroken and it was hard to tell. She turned to Charlie, who did not flinch, but lowered his eyes slightly, avoiding her gaze. It was this lowering of the eyes that in Grace's mind constituted an admission of guilt.

But if that were an admission, it was quickly withdrawn. 'I didn't bite him,' Charlie muttered. '*He* bit *me*. I just pushed him because he's bad.'

Grace turned to Magnus. 'Did you bite Charlie, Magnus?'

This question was greeted with outrage and a scream of denial. Grace looked back at Charlie. 'He says he didn't.'

'Magnus is a big liar,' said Charlie. 'He tells fibs all the time.'

Grace drew in her breath. There was no doubt in her mind: Charlie had bitten Magnus. The older boy's studied coolness was just too much. Had he been innocent, he would have refuted the allegation straight away, and with feeling. False accusation always brings a note of anger in the response it draws. He had done it.

Grace wagged a finger at Charlie. 'You listen to me, Charlie. If you bite Magnus – even a little bite – you'll be sorry. Do you hear me?'

Charlie looked away, affecting indifference.

'Are you listening to me?' she repeated.

Again, there was indifference.

Grace made up her mind. 'Now,' she said. 'You tell me this: how would you feel if somebody bigger than you bit you?'

He shrugged. The pedestrian crossing light had turned green, and now was red again.

'Don't care,' said Charlie defiantly, adding, 'You smell.'

Something moved within Grace. Deep in her memory, overlaid by the passage of years, a moment of raw hurt surfaced. She was back in the playground, in her tenth year, and she was being mocked by a small band of girls, her enemies of the time, who ridiculed her for the threadbare school uniform she was obliged to wear, a handed-down hand-me-down that proclaimed her parents' straitened circumstances – there was no money; there never was – and the girls who teased her had clothes that had belonged to nobody but them, and expensive ribbons; and one of them, her principal tormentor, a pigtailed girl with a retroussé nose, had jeered and called out, in that sing-song tone that is the hallmark of children's taunts the world over, 'Smelly Grace in her smelly dress.' And that came back now, suddenly, unexpectedly.

Grace grabbed Charlie's hand, on impulse, and gave it a nip with her teeth. It was not a strong nip, but it was a nip.

Releasing the hand, she said, 'There, you see. You don't like it, do you?'

Charlie stared at Grace, his eyes wide. Then he let out a howl of protest. Magnus looked on, equally surprised.

'So that settles that,' said Grace. 'If you bite anybody, you'll be bitten back.' She paused. 'So now, let's get home and we can have some bread and honey and start behaving like civilised beings once more.' The children would forget about it. They never thought about these things for long; they were always having little spats with one another and then, the next moment, everything was back to normal and sweetness and light were restored.

They walked back largely in silence, with only the occasional sniffle from Charlie, whose pride had been severely dented by the summary justice meted out on the street. As they approached the house, though, he looked up at Grace and said, 'I'm going to tell Mummy you bit me.'

Grace stopped. She was already regretting her impetuous response. She had never raised a hand to the children – they were not hers to discipline, anyway – and now she had *bitten* one of them. She could hardly believe it of herself. It had been an ill-thought-out, knee-jerk response, the product of a painful memory and a sudden urge to punish. She had betrayed Isabel's trust. She may have meant well; she may have thought it necessary to teach him a simple lesson about life – that bad behaviour had painful consequences. But you did not do it this way. *You did not bite children. You did not.*

Grace panicked. She would lose her job – in ignominy. She would be utterly shamed. She could not allow that to happen, and yet there seemed to be no way in which this disastrous outcome could be averted. Unless ... Bending down, she whispered to Charlie, 'I'm very sorry, Charlie. Let's just forget about what happened.'

The boy glared at her, but said nothing. They finished the journey in silence, which was only interrupted by a muttered 'Witch!' from Charlie, but not so loud that anybody could hear him.

12

Charlie said nothing about the contretemps to Isabel when she came back to the house later that afternoon. Grace was there when Isabel came into the room and brightly asked Charlie about his school lunch and also whether anything had happened. Charlie glanced briefly at Grace, as if to prolong her anxiety, but then he turned back to face his mother and mumbled, 'Nothing. Sausages for lunch.'

'Sausages!' exclaimed Isabel. 'How imaginative.'

'And peas,' he added.

'Well, that was a good meal,' said Isabel breezily. 'Both of those will make you strong.'

'I'm very strong already,' said Charlie.

'So you are,' said Isabel. 'You are just like young Hercules. I shall tell you about him one day.' She would not mention the snake in the Greek hero's crib and his decisive way of dealing with it; she would not mention that just yet.

Charlie said nothing, and Grace breathed a sigh of relief. Later on, though, she made up her mind to tell Isabel what had happened. She did not want to keep anything from Isabel – they had always been frank with one another – and her decision to confess brought her relief. Now, as she arrived at the Masonic Hall for the meeting of the Second Circle of Light, she was able to put the thought of that afternoon's incident out of her mind and concentrate on the programme ahead. Most members of the group were already there when she arrived, and she exchanged greetings with several of them as she helped herself to the cup of tea that always preceded what the leader of the group called *the onset of the light*.

Grace found herself talking to her friend Jennifer, who had, like her, migrated from the old group to the new. Jennifer worked in a small jewellery shop in Morningside, owned by her sister, who lived in Portugal. Jennifer had pursued an interest in spiritualism after she had an out-of-body experience after giving birth in the maternity ward of the Infirmary. She had been convinced that she was looking down on her bed from above, and that her late mother was standing beside her, explaining that it was not quite time to leave and that she should return to her mortal body for the time being. 'Those were the exact words, Grace,' Jennifer had said. 'You don't think I'm making this up, do you? Some people do, you know. They think this is all imagination – a dream, or whatever. But I was absolutely awake, I swear I was. I was awake.'

Grace had assured her that she was the last person to express scepticism about that sort of thing. 'I completely believe you,' she said. 'And you're really lucky to have had that happen to you. Not everyone has that sort of experience.'

'I asked the doctors whether I had technically died,' Jennifer said. 'They looked at me and one of them said, "No, you can't have. You're here, aren't you?" And there was no further discussion.'

'There's nothing like a closed mind,' said Grace. 'Some people only want to hear what they want to hear.'

Now, over her cup of tea, Jennifer was telling Grace about a brooch she was making. 'It's a thistle,' she said. 'The top bit will be made of crystal and the body will be silver. It's not going to be too expensive.'

They talked about that, and then moved on to discuss a string of pearls that Grace had inherited from an aunt in Glasgow that needed restringing. Jennifer could do that, she said, and she would make no charge for it. 'It's very simple,' she said, 'but you have to do it properly.'

And then the leader made her way over towards them, accompanied by a short, rather fussy-looking man.

'This is Mr Armstrong,' the leader said. And then, turning to Grace and Jennifer, 'I'm going to leave you with these two excellent ladies, Phillip. We'll start in ten minutes or so.'

Grace looked at Mr Armstrong. He was somewhere in his fifties, she thought, and he was wearing a suit that looked as if it was several sizes too small for him. She noticed that there was dandruff on his shoulders, and that the suede shoes he was wearing were stained across the toecap. You have to treat suede before you wear it, she thought. You have to waterproof it or your shoes will end up looking like these. She almost felt inclined to tell him, to whisper to him that if he wanted to avoid further discolouration of his shoes, he should do something about waterproofing them. It was elementary, really – but perhaps it was the sort of thing that men never really thought about. They don't care about their shoes in the way that we women care about them, thought Grace.

Mr Armstrong nodded to the leader and then turned to Grace and Jennifer.

'I must say,' he began, 'that this is a very fine hall for your Circle meetings.'

He spoke with a pronounced Glaswegian accent, Grace noticed, and he had halitosis. She felt almost embarrassed to notice this – it was not his fault, just as his dandruff was not his fault – but one could hardly not be aware of it.

Jennifer had recoiled slightly when he began to speak. Now she made an effort, and smiled broadly. 'I gather you're our medium this evening. Thanks for coming all the way from . . .'

She trailed off, and he provided the rest of the sentence. 'From Motherwell. We have a small group there, but an active one.'

Motherwell was just outside Glasgow – a town associated with heavy industries that had now disappeared. It was not the most glamorous of Scotland's towns, but Grace had cousins there, and she mentioned that now. 'I don't think you will have met them,' she said to Mr Armstrong. 'They are strong doubters – about everything, as far as I can see.'

'There are many such people,' said Mr Armstrong, taking a sip of his tea. 'But tell me, what do you ladies do?'

Grace explained that she was a housekeeper, and that Jennifer made jewellery.

'And I repair watches too,' added Jennifer. 'That's an important part of my work.'

Mr Armstrong smiled at her. 'I am sure it makes you punctual.' Then he asked, 'Are you the only jeweller in the family? Sometimes it's a family profession, isn't it?'

'My parents were jewellers too,' she said. 'And my sister. She owns the business, actually, but lives in Portugal now.'

'I see,' said Mr Armstrong. 'And your parents are long retired?'

'They died some time ago,' said Jennifer.

Mr Armstrong now turned to Grace. 'How did you become involved in the movement?' he asked.

Grace shrugged. 'Somebody brought me along to a meeting a long time ago. You know how it is. I thought it interesting.'

'And it is, isn't it?' said Mr Armstrong. 'If only people knew what contact with another dimension adds to our lives, but they seem determined to ignore the evidence. Determined.' He shook his head sadly before continuing, 'Oh well, we shall see what this evening brings. You never know. I am constantly surprised by the sheer number of guides who wish to make contact with us. They are there, right there, simply waiting for the right moment.'

Jennifer suddenly leaned forward and said in a lowered voice, 'We heard from Mary, Queen of Scots herself the other day. She was here.'

Mr Armstrong looked impressed. 'She has never been to Motherwell,' he said, sounding slightly regretful. 'I suppose she knew Edinburgh better, even if it had unhappy associations for her.'

'She referred to the killing of Rizzio,' Jennifer went on. 'I think that Darnley was mixed up in that. Her own husband. It was shameful.'

'A very bad thing,' said Mr Armstrong. 'I wouldn't be surprised if she were still angry about it.'

'She didn't say,' said Jennifer.

Mr Armstrong looked thoughtful. 'Sometimes they don't. They don't necessarily tell us everything. There is a veil that separates our world from theirs, a curtain, and most of the time we get no more than a brief glimpse of what lies beyond it.'

Mr Armstrong finished his tea and Jennifer took the empty cup from him. 'I'll look after this.'

'You're very kind.' And then he drew her aside. 'That man

164

over there – the one near the door. He looks rather unhappy. Do you know who he is?'

Jennifer followed the medium's gaze. 'He's called Donald – I'm not sure what his other name is. I did know it, but I've forgotten. Unhappy? Yes, I think he is. He lost his wife a couple of years ago. She was head teacher of a school just outside town. I think he's still grieving.'

'So sad,' said Mr Armstrong, lowering his gaze. 'So sad. But I think your leader wants us to begin. Look.'

The leader was marshalling people into their seats. 'The light is about to arrive,' she announced. 'Please make yourselves comfortable, everybody, and then the light will commence.' She called across the room to Mr Armstrong. 'Phillip, please come and sit up here where everybody can see you. That's right. Over here.'

They took their seats. Grace sat with Jennifer on her right and a young man with long hair on her left. She had met the young man before, but he seemed in awe of her and had volunteered very little information about himself other than his name, which was Faolan. 'It's Gaelic for wolf,' he had whispered, as if divulging a secret. Directly opposite them in the circle sat the leader and Mr Armstrong, the latter on a slightly raised chair.

'The onset of light is with us,' announced the leader. 'We are now ready – our hearts are open.'

In the silence that followed, most closed their eyes. Grace did not; she preferred to watch the medium, and now she saw that he was glancing around the circle, as if to take in who was present. She looked down sharply so that he should not see her staring at him.

Mr Armstrong broke the silence. 'Dear friends,' he began. 'There is in this room a good energy. It is there, and I can

165

feel it within me. We draw now on that energy that we have created by our presence this evening to call upon those on the other side who may wish to speak to us. We are open to their thoughts and words. We acknowledge their presence amongst us. We extend our hands in love.'

Grace drew in her breath. This was the moment that she found most moving – the moment of invocation. And he was so right, she thought, to talk of extending hands. That was precisely how she viewed it – a reaching out.

There was renewed silence. Somebody in the circle cleared his throat – a stifled cough. A patch of darkness moved across a wall, but it was only the shadow cast by the head of one of the members. The lights should be dimmed, thought Grace – that was always conducive to the presence of spirit.

Now Mr Armstrong spoke. His voice seemed to have a different quality now – it was higher, and not as loud as it had been before. And something else was different, too: the West of Scotland accent had been replaced by something different – something not unlike an Irish burr. One should not be surprised by that, Grace thought: we had no idea of the extent of dis-embodiment on the other side, and voice might well remain in its earthly form. How had Mary, Queen of Scots sounded? She had said so little, but everybody present was agreed that she had spoken with what would now be called a Morningside accent, an accent peculiar to south Edinburgh and noted for its exaggerated vowels. The first person, *I*, was pronounced as a simple letter *a* in Morningside. Mary had sounded a bit like that, and yet, should she not have spoken with a French accent because of her upbringing in the French court? Somebody had asked that, but had been silenced by discouraging looks from those who had felt honoured that Mary should have chosen to be amongst them, even if only for a very brief spell.

166

Now Mr Armstrong said, 'I am aware of a presence that wishes to speak to one of us. There is a very strong presence.'

This caused a ripple of movement – of looking up, of tensing of limbs, of anticipation mirrored in the set of mouths.

'Yes,' continued Mr Armstrong, 'there is one here beside me. She is a lady of good bearing. She is surrounded by light. She has a message for one of us, although I am not sure who it is. She is standing behind the light and I cannot see if she is pointing. But I can hear her voice, and she is saying something about the carrying on of work that has already been started.' He paused. The silence that followed his words was complete. Then he continued, his voice becoming slightly fainter so that people strained to hear. 'She says that the work of adorning others is good work and brings great joy. She is happy that it is continuing on earth now that she is in the realm of spirit.'

Grace felt Jennifer give a start. Snatching a glance to her side, she saw that her friend was sitting bolt upright now, her eyes wide open. The expression on her face was one of astonishment – and of delight.

Mr Armstrong was looking up at the ceiling. Now he smiled – and brushed dandruff off his right shoulder.

'That lady is now retreating back into the realm of spirit,' he said, his normal voice returning. 'But there is another. There is a man here – a tall man with glasses.' He waited, and then said, 'Does anybody perhaps recognise this man with glasses?'

A woman a few places down from Grace looked up. 'Does he have red hair?'

Mr Armstrong closed his eyes. 'I'm not sure. No ... but wait, yes, I think he does. Yes, he has red hair. And he's saying something: he says you should not worry. He says that the time for worry has passed.'

The woman sat back in her seat. Her hand went up to wipe at her eyes. Grace looked away. Tears were common at these meetings, and it was not surprising, she thought: after all, these were moments of reunion.

Mr Armstrong smiled. He seemed pleased with what had transpired so far. Now he said, 'And I am receiving another message. I am not sure who it is for – but I think that the person for whom it is intended will know. There is somebody here . . . I can see her now . . . yes, I can see her quite clearly. She is surrounded by children. She is showing the children something – I cannot tell what it is, but they are flocking about her. Perhaps she is their teacher – yes, I think she is a teacher of children who have crossed over. She says that she wants you to know that she is happy and that you must be happy for her. She does not want you to be unhappy. She says there is no need for that – no need at all.'

Grace frowned. She, at least, knew who that message was for, because she remembered Mr Armstrong enquiring about Donald. Jennifer had said something about his wife having been a teacher – Grace was sure of it – and so he would have known that detail. People were always suggesting that mediums simply used information they already had – it was a common criticism made by doubters. Grace was no doubter, but at the same time she knew that there were those whose powers of mediumship were weak and who might resort to trickery in order to boost their reputations. She had not been too impressed with Mr Armstrong's manner, and it was possible that he was one of these marginal mediums. That irritated her. It was a waste of everybody's time to have people like that spouting meaningless generalisations.

But then Mr Armstrong closed his eyes again and raised his voice. 'There is something else,' he said. 'There is somebody here who is trying to pass a message to one of our number. This is an important message. It is very important.'

They waited. Even Grace, who was about to write off Mr Armstrong, found herself paying attention.

'The message is for one who is about to make a mistake,' Mr Armstrong intoned. 'It is a warning, I think.'

This deepened the almost tangible sense of anticipation that prevailed round the circle. It was rare to receive a warning, and it would certainly be heeded.

'It is very important,' Mr Armstrong continued, 'not to intervene in those matters that do not concern us. Spirit says that we each have our portion of the garden to tend and must not stray over into that part which belongs to another.'

Grace had been staring at her hands, which she had folded on her lap. Now she looked up, and saw that Mr Armstrong was looking straight at her. She turned away; it might have been coincidence, but when she looked back at him, he still had his eyes fixed on her. She felt her heart beating hard. That message had been for her – there could be no doubt about it. It was as personal as if it had been written out and placed in an envelope bearing her name, complete with a first-class stamp.

She had said nothing to Mr Armstrong that would have enabled him to know about her conversation with Jamie and her offer of help. And yet there was no doubt but that the medium was warning her very specifically not to interfere in the business of others. She shook her head, as if to free herself of these disquieting thoughts. If Mr Armstrong knew nothing about that, then was this a warning from the other side? What other explanation could there be – unless it was simple coincidence and the warning was no more than a generic observation. But why, then, would he have been looking at her so intently?

Mr Armstrong, who had been standing while speaking, now

took a step back and sat down in his chair. This was the signal for the leader to take over. She thanked him for his messages – 'every one of them pertinent and helpful,' she said – and looked forward to his imminent return for future sessions.

Jennifer had laid a hand on Grace's forearm. 'Well,' she whispered. 'That was quite something, wasn't it?'

Grace nodded.

'And what he said at the end was very thought-provoking,' Jennifer continued. 'It's only too easy to get caught up in matters that don't concern you.' She paused before adding, 'And then regret it.'

Grace glanced at her. Had Jennifer intended this to be a none-too-subtle underlining of the warning? She thought this unlikely, as there was no reason for Jennifer to know about the business with Jamie. She stood up. 'I have to get home,' she said. 'I've got a lot to do.'

Jennifer smiled and said she looked forward to seeing Grace at the next meeting. 'There's a woman coming over from Ireland,' she said. 'From Cork. I heard she's very good. Have you heard of her? Maeve-Catriona O'Farrell. She's written a book on near-death experiences.'

Grace nodded. She had heard of Maeve-Catriona O'Farrell, who had not one, but two near-death experiences, but she did not feel like talking about her now. 'I have to get home,' she repeated.

As she left the hall, she threw a quick glance at the far end where Mr Armstrong was standing in a small knot of people that included the leader and one or two members of the committee. He was looking at her. Again, it might have been coincidence – it probably was – but it disconcerted her. In her view it made it even clearer that if the warning was a genuine one, then it was undoubtedly directed at her and she should take it seriously. The whole point about the world of spirit was that it was beyond time. Past, present and future were human inventions, applicable in our limited realm, but not necessarily binding elsewhere. It was perfectly possible – indeed it was an utterly normal occurrence – for a future danger to be picked up in the world of spirit and communicated to us as a warning. And there was an important difference between an exhortation, an admonition, and a warning. The last of these was a serious matter and should not be taken lightly, and Grace would not do that.

She left the Masonic Hall. At nine-fifteen, it was still light, but the air was fresh and Grace donned the cardigan she had brought with her – a Fair Isle knit that she had bought the previous year on a trip to Shetland. It was hand-knitted, in the traditional pattern of those parts, muted colours worked into the elaborate diamond and arrow designs that were said to have been used to identify drowned fishermen given up by the sea. Isabel had decried that as a myth, and pointed out to Grace that the same thing was believed of Arran sweaters and the jerseys knitted by other women on other coasts. 'A lot of the things we believe in, Grace,' she had said, 'are simply not true – like the Loch Ness monster, for instance.' That had been accompanied by an intense look that Grace had interpreted as a sceptical comment on her spiritualist meetings, for which she knew Isabel had little time. But Grace was tolerant – how did we know what lurked in the depths of Loch Ness; how could we be so *sure*? Would Isabel swim in Loch Ness, alone, by night? Would she? So she simply quoted back her favourite line from *Hamlet*: 'There are more things in heaven and earth, Horatio, than are dreamt of in your philosophy.' Then they had both laughed; it was Grace's standard response to any expression of doubt – a knowing hint at the limits of knowledge.

The Fair Isle jersey was a favourite garment of hers, and donning it now, as she began to walk down Thistle Street, gave her the feeling of security that comes from wearing familiar clothing, that made even a cardigan a suit of light armour. The city was quiet, and although she had not lingered at the meeting, where people would often have a second, post-séance cup of tea before departing, she now felt in no rush to get home. She had been discomforted by Mr Armstrong's last message, and she felt that a stroll back to her flat was what she needed to settle the vague sense of anxiety with which his warning had left her.

She made her way down the hill to Gloucester Lane, a sharply descending road that emerged in the middle of the two abutting Georgian terraces further down towards Stockbridge. The lane was cobbled, and one had to be careful to avoid getting a heel stuck in between the stone setts that made its surface. It was also poorly lit, and in the dark nights of winter Grace never felt entirely comfortable walking down it, preferring to make her way down the broad sweep of India Street only a short distance away to the east. But this was dusk on a summer evening and there were birds in the sky above, swallows darting against a backdrop of washed-out blue. She felt safe here, surrounded by architecture that was the very embodiment of reason – sturdy, well proportioned, inhabited by reliable people.

She became aware that somebody was behind her. She was not sure how this sense of another arose – the figure was too far away for her to hear footsteps, but when she half turned she saw him, right up at the top of the lane, walking down towards her. She felt a sudden sense of unease. There was something familiar about the figure, although she had seen very little of it. Now she realised who it was: Mr Armstrong. She was certain of it.

She increased her pace. Now she could hear the man's foot steps – the clatter of hard leather soles against the stone of the setts. She did not turn round, but continued to walk swiftly, at just below the pace of a run. Suddenly she found herself level with the entrance to a set of mews houses – a square that opened up to the left, around which a series of old coach houses and stables had been converted to modern flats. On impulse she turned sharply and ran into the square. There were lights on in one or two of the houses and she briefly toyed with the idea of ringing the doorbell of one of these. She was safe now, as even if Mr Armstrong had been following her – and she realised, now, that there was every likelihood that he had not been doing that – she was no longer alone. There were people in the houses; they would see whatever happened under their noses in the square.

But then she saw that one of the houses had a garage on its lower level and that the garage door was slightly ajar. Without waiting, she crossed the square, opened the door further and slipped inside. There was a smell of petrol and a musty odour of old hessian – the smell of a garage. She stood just inside, and watched through a chink at the side of the door as Mr Armstrong came into the square, stopped and looked about him. Now she was sure he had been following her.

She held her breath. The medium had taken off his glasses and was polishing them with a white handkerchief. Then he replaced the glasses and looked in her direction. Had he seen her? He must have done, as he now began to advance across the centre of the square. In a few seconds he would be at the garage.

She acted quickly, slamming the door shut. As she did this, the tongue of a sprung lock clicked into place. Whoever was outside would not be able to get in now. She was safe.

She thought she heard breathing outside, but could not be sure. She was standing in complete darkness, but she could tell that the door was being tested. There was a creak as whoever was outside pulled on the handle, and a creak when, realising it was locked, he released it.

Grace swallowed.

She heard a voice outside.

'Hello?'

It was him.

She stopped breathing. She could not breathe.

'Hello in there?'

Something scuttled away inside the garage – a mouse, she thought, but it made her start.

'What do you want?' It was her own voice, but it sounded as if it came from somebody else. She had not intended to speak.

'Don't be afraid. I mean you no harm.'

She waited.

'I just wanted to tell you that what I said at the meeting was meant for you.'

She listened.

'You see, the world of spirit was very clear about it. It wanted you to know. It was concerned.'

She opened her mouth to speak. Her lips were dry. 'Why?' It was all she could manage.

'Because they think you're in danger.' He paused. 'That's all I wanted to say to you.'

Thinking she might collapse, she reached out to hold on to something. It was the wing of a car, and it was cold to the touch.

'I have to catch a train back to Glasgow,' the voice said. 'I didn't mean to alarm you. I'm sorry if I frightened you.'

She managed, 'I'm not frightened.' She said this while

thinking: I'm cowering behind a stranger's garage door, my heart racing . . .

For a few moments he was silent, then he said, 'Good. I must go now.'

She waited for a few minutes before she opened the garage door. She had heard his retreating footsteps and was confident that he was no longer there. Closing the garage door behind her, she started the walk back to her flat. She knew what she had to do. She would speak to Jamie the next day and tell him that she had reconsidered her position and would unfortunately not be able to help him. More than that, she would try to persuade him not to interfere himself, because a warning is sometimes broader in its effect than one might imagine, and may apply to others than those to whom it is initially addressed. That could mean it applied to Jamie as well; and Isabel, too, come to think of it, although there would be no persuading her, Grace thought, with regret. She was fond of Isabel – how could one not be? – but sometimes she wished she would be less of a philosopher and more of an ordinary person; like me, thought Grace.

13

That evening, while Grace was at the Second Circle of Light in Thistle Street, Isabel was in her kitchen paging through a recipe book, while Jamie, ever the patient father, was reading aloud, for the second time that evening, the adventures of Babar the Francophone elephant. Babar had left the land of the elephants and had arrived, with scant regard to the constraints of geography, in Paris, where he encountered the evident benefits of French civilisation. The boys could hear the story time and time again, ready to complain about any excision of text, any skipping of detail, although the fate of Babar's mother had been deleted all along; in due course, Jamie knew, when they were in a position to read the book for themselves, they would discover what happened to her – how she had been shot by a hunter – but that would be later in their lives, when they might be better equipped to cope with tragedy.

It was Isabel's turn to cook and, after some thought and research, she had decided on two courses from a recipe book

Jamie had given her for her last birthday, along with an emerald ring on the inside of which he had had inscribed her initials and the date. The book was *A Taste of Scotland's Islands*, and Isabel had tried a number of recipes before. Now she had alighted on a mushroom risotto and a pudding – a safe choice for Jamie, who liked, she had discovered, reassuring food. The risotto called for Hebridean Black Pudding, which Isabel declined to use, on the grounds that she could not face black pudding in any context, and neither, she knew, could Jamie. It was popular in Scotland, but the thought of eating congealed pig's blood – which is what black pudding effectively was – did not appeal. As a result, the risotto, like the Babar story, had been shorn of one of its elements, but would stand quite well enough on the remaining ingredients, which included a liberal helping of truffle oil.

But even that was not without controversy. Jamie loved truffles and relished anything in which their characteristic earthy pungency was evident. As a result, he would readily dowse almost anything with truffle-scented olive oil, would drizzle the same oil over potatoes or scrambled eggs, and would spread white truffle paste onto truffle-imbued wheat crackers. Had truffle-scented aftershave lotion been available, he would undoubtedly have been a regular user, or so Isabel had playfully suggested, only to discover that he rather liked the idea of that.

The problem with truffles, though, lay in their ridiculous price: few could afford the eye-watering prices that were paid for the awkward lumps of fungus detected by the pigs and hounds of the truffle hunters. Their scarcity, though, had been a challenge to the chemists, who had come up with truffle oil in response, which, in many cases, was simply doctored olive oil, and which imparted the smell of the fungus to the food with which it was served. It was not based on truffles, though, but was 2,4-dithiapentane, a molecule that smelled of truffle. Truffle experts had nothing but contempt for this substitute, considering it an olfactory fake that desensitised the palate to the real thing. Jamie, though, would have none of that. 'I like it,' he said. 'And is there anything actually *wrong* in liking a fake?' His question had resolved the issue, at least for their household: truffle oil, even if it was anathema to some, had its place on the oil and vinegar shelf in their kitchen.

Now, with the boys settled and Babar returned to Celesteville, Jamie came into the kitchen, sniffed at the air, and exclaimed, 'Truffles!'

'Ersatz,' said Isabel. 'As usual. 2,4-dithiapentane for dinner tonight.'

Jamie sighed. 'I know, I know. But there's more to it than that. There are other chemicals too.' He paused. 'Carefully chosen.'

'Look.' She pointed to a pile of chestnut mushrooms on a chopping board. 'At least the mushrooms are real.'

Jamie sat down. Isabel had already poured herself a glass of white wine, and now she poured one for him too. They had wine on Tuesdays, Fridays and Saturdays, and tended to abstinence on the remaining days of the week – a compromise, Isabel felt, between sobriety and self-indulgence. And making Tuesday a wine day had the additional effect, Isabel thought, of sanctifying a day that would otherwise be unremarkable. Friday and Saturday required no help – they were days invested, she felt, with the warm glow of completion: the week had been survived, and the weekend either lay ahead or was already there – whereas Tuesday was nothing special.

'Babar,' said Jamie, and sighed.

'Again?'

He nodded. 'I am very pro-elephant. I am particularly

pro-elephants that wear green jackets and spats. I adore Pom, Flora and Alexander. However, I do feel that I have been there rather a lot recently.'

'Give them something new,' suggested Isabel. 'What's wrong with Winnie the Pooh?'

'I've tried, but there are howls of protest. Babar is the flavour of the month.'

'Like truffle oil?'

He smiled weakly. 'I'm hungry,' he said. And then, taking a sip of his wine, he continued, 'Charlie said something at bath time.'

Isabel started to chop the mushrooms. 'Oh, yes?'

Jamie frowned. 'It was very odd. He suddenly looked at me and said, "Grace bit me." Those were his exact words: "Grace bit me."'

Isabel put down her knife. 'Highly unlikely. Are you sure?'

Jamie nodded. 'He seemed serious. So I asked him what he meant, and he said, "Grace bit me on the hand."'

Isabel sat down. 'There's been a biting issue at school. I was going to talk to you about it. Miss Young said that Charlie had bitten somebody. In fact, it was that little boy called Rory. You know the one? His father's—'

'The dentist? The one married to that woman with peroxide hair?'

'Yes. But when he asked Rory whether Charlie had bitten him, he denied it. I thought it was probably some sort of playground scrap – nothing to do with real biting. But Miss Young seemed to be quite serious about it. She wanted me to talk to Charlie. She even made some remark about violent children, which I thought was a bit over the top.'

'Well,' said Jamie. 'Now he says that Grace bit *him*.'

Isabel made a face. 'Children distort things.'

179

'Of course they do. And we encourage them to think that elephants wear jackets and speak French. We can hardly be surprised.' He took another sip of his wine. 'But then Magnus piped up. He said, "Grace bit Charlie's nose."'

'Oh really,' said Isabel. 'They were having you on.'

'Except that Charlie then said, "Yes, I meant my nose. She bit my nose. And I hate her now."'

'He doesn't,' said Isabel simply. 'He adores Grace. They both do.'

'That's what I've always thought,' said Jamie. 'And I think you're right. But why would they suddenly accuse her of this? It seems a bit odd.'

Isabel replied that a child's mind was capable of very odd conclusions. 'You know what they're like.'

'Yes,' said Jamie. 'But . . . But it just seemed odd to me. They both looked serious when they spoke about it.'

When this conversation had begun, Isabel had been bemused rather than concerned. Children were inventive and could easily confuse the active and passive tenses – thus might a biter become the bitten. This was bizarre, whichever way you viewed it: Charlie had clearly not been bitten on the nose by anybody, let alone by Grace, whom Isabel trusted unquestioningly with the children. Grace had never so much as given them a minor tap on the wrist – even under the sort of severe provocation that a toddler in full voice can offer. That she should suddenly bite Charlie was unthinkable, particularly when he himself stood under fresh and recent accusation of biting. The psychologists would have a word for this, she thought. Was it transference, or was that just applied to situations where people directed feelings about one person to an entirely different person? This was more a case of transferring authorship of an act to another, which was not quite the same thing. Perhaps Charlie had bitten Grace – which was possible, Isabel supposed, given recent accusations – but then, feeling guilty, had sought to transfer the blame to her. Or perhaps he was aware that he was under investigation, so to speak, for biting, and thought that by pointing the finger at Grace he might deflect any unwanted attention in her direction. There was a simple name for that – framing – which was widely understood. Charlie might be trying to frame Grace, Isabel thought, in order to throw the forces of law and order (me, Miss Young) off the scent.

She became aware that Jamie had asked her a question.

'Isabel?'

'Yes.'

'Well, what do you think?'

She asked him to repeat his question.

'I asked you whether you could think of any reason for him to make this all up?'

She shrugged. 'Guilt? Let's say that he bit Rory—'

Jamie interrupted her. 'But Rory says he didn't.'

'Intimidation of witnesses, and so on.'

Jamie laughed. 'Oh, come on, Isabel. You're making it sound like a mafia drama. Isn't that a bit extreme?'

'But that's exactly what it is,' Isabel replied. 'Down among the five-year-olds. It's brutal down there. The law of the jungle. Palermo, Naples – those places have nothing on Primary One. Nothing.'

Jamie was unconvinced. 'I think he's making it up. Look at the way the site of the injury shifted from hand to nose. His nose, for heaven's sake! How could she have bitten him on the nose?'

'That might have been his way of exaggerating the injury,' said Isabel.

Jamie stared at her. 'I wonder whether we're up against something more peculiar here. What's that condition where people make up an illness?'

'Munchausen's Syndrome?'

'Yes,' said Jamie. 'That. Perhaps it's a version of Munchausen's. It could be a way of getting attention. If you say to somebody that you've been bitten on the nose, then you're bound to get sympathy.'

Isabel thought about this. Jamie could be right, and if he was, then the whole matter could be dealt with in the same way as one would deal with any other attention-seeking behaviour. The behaviour itself could be ignored, but love and attention could be otherwise lavished on the attention-seeker. And love, after all, was the universal panacea, the balm that could heal virtually any hurt. No child ever suffered from too much love ... She stopped herself. No, that was not true. You *could* give children too much love and give them a false idea of themselves – the idea that they could do no wrong, because they would always be loved by Mother. Love had to be tempered with a certain amount of holding to account. I may love you, but I am still capable of seeing your faults; in other words, don't think you're perfect.

Jamie had a question. 'Are you going to speak to Grace?'

Isabel looked thoughtful. 'I don't think I should,' she said at last. 'For one thing, she can be touchy.'

Jamie nodded. Isabel was right, as he had discovered on a number of occasions where he had spoken tactlessly and Grace had taken offence – sometimes, he thought, unreasonably. Her huffs did not last, though, and an injured silence of ten minutes might be the extent of the reaction. But he was careful in how he put things to her. And he did not judge her harshly: her position in the household was that of employee and you should always bear in mind, he reminded himself, that employees might feel vulnerable to the whim of those who employed them.

In essence, it was a simple question of decent behaviour. There were those who considered decency to be an outmoded virtue – rather old-fashioned, like turn-ups on trousers or shoes with laces, or addressing people as Mr or Mrs – but decency still counted for something and when you saw it, you knew it for what it was. Jamie had seen it first hand when he had been invited to play in a quartet at a concert in a large house in the Scottish Borders. The owner of the house was a man who could have been very grand – he had the means – and yet he was not grand at all; he was, by contrast, a *great* man, which Jamie realised was a very different thing. And what made him a great man was his kindness and courtesy to every last person with whom he came into contact, whatever their position in human hierarchies. Jamie had witnessed the way he spoke to the staff who were looking after the guests, addressing each by name, making sure that everybody felt appreciated. That, thought Jamie, was the acid test. If you treated those in menial positions with the same courtesy and consideration that you gave those who were more elevated, then you passed the test. If you did not – if you paid less attention to those who were relatively unimportant – then you failed.

He brought himself back to what Isabel had said. He agreed with her; it was highly likely that Grace would take offence were she to be accused of biting Charlie. Who wouldn't?

'I think we should leave it be,' Isabel went on. 'I'll watch the situation. At an appropriate moment I'll talk to him about not biting people, as I promised to. But frankly, it's best ignored.'

Jamie agreed. 'Funny little things,' he said.

'The boys? Yes, they are, aren't they? Their minds are full

of heaven knows what. Odd beliefs. Peculiar notions. It's all very mixed up until . . . until when? When do they start to be aware of things like the feelings of others? Seven? Eight?'

'Twenty-eight,' said Jamie. And when Isabel laughed, he continued, 'No, I mean it. There's a school of thought that holds that most men don't really grow up until round about then. Women are different. They're mature much younger, but men still do stupid things until . . .'

'Sixty-five,' suggested Isabel, with a smile.

Jamie thought about this. 'Men of sixty-five can still behave irresponsibly,' he said. 'Some men of that age still have affairs. They still leave their wives.' He paused. 'They go off with younger women.'

Isabel sighed, and started to measure out the arborio rice for the risotto. 'Men,' she said. Then she said, 'I've been thinking.'

Jamie waited.

'I've been thinking about our conversation the other day. When we agreed that I'd . . .'

'Look into this business with Laurence?' prompted Jamie.

'Yes. And you said you'd do something about that poor family.'

She poured the rice into a saucepan, and then looked up to fix Jamie with an apologetic look. 'It was a bad idea,' she said.

Jamie grinned. 'Really bad,' he agreed. 'I was going to talk to you about it.'

Isabel held her hands open in a gesture of relief. 'I don't know why I thought it made sense. It doesn't. I should have realised that you can't pass on your responsibilities just like that.' She paused. 'Not that it's been a complete waste of time. I have something to tell you. I had lunch in The Chaumer.'

'Oh yes?'

'He was there,' she said. 'Your conductor – he turned up.'

Jamie looked interested. 'And?'

'He wasn't alone. He had a young woman with him.'

Jamie nodded. 'He usually does. Late twenties-ish? Quite tall?'

Isabel nodded.

'Could be her,' said Jamie.

'Who?'

'His girlfriend. The person we think he intends to give the job to.'

Now Isabel said, 'I know her name, though. I heard him say it.'

Jamie raised an eyebrow. 'Yes?'

'Annette,' said Isabel. 'I heard him call her Annette.'

Jamie frowned. 'Are you sure? Annette?'

'That's the name I overheard. And there's something else: I noticed her eyes. They were an unusual colour – quite striking.'

Jamie was silent as he absorbed what Isabel had said. Then he said, 'Grey?'

'Yes,' said Isabel. 'Almost.'

'Yes, very light blue. You could call them grey?' He paused. 'An English accent? Did you hear her speak?'

'Yes. I didn't think she was Scottish.'

'Rather posh?'

Isabel shrugged. 'A bit. Not too grating. Not too affected. But yes, if I had to guess, I'd say she had been expensively educated somewhere.'

'That's her,' said Jamie suddenly. 'That's Annette Jamieson. It must be her. And she's not English, actually – she comes from Fife somewhere. She was at Fettes, I think.' Fettes was an exclusive boarding school in Edinburgh.

'Then she went down to the Leeds Conservatoire,'

Jamie went on. 'She came back and did a year in the Music Department at Glasgow University – a master's of some sort. She's a really good player.'

Isabel listened to this. If Annette Jamieson was a really good player, then the person who really deserved to get the job must be exceptional. She asked Jamie about this, and was surprised when he shook his head vigorously.

'No,' he said. 'She's not the one who doesn't deserve the job, she's the one who does.'

'I'm sorry,' said Isabel. 'You're losing me here. This Annette Jamieson is having an affair with the conductor. Is that right?'

'No, it isn't. She's the player who *isn't* going to be appointed. She deserves the job, but she isn't going to get it, even if she's on the shortlist. The person he's having an affair with is called Athene. She's not nearly as good a player as Annette.'

Isabel struggled with this. 'So this lunch they were having together was . . . what? Just lunch?'

Jamie hesitated. 'I suppose it must have been. Perhaps they were talking about . . . Well, I don't know.' An idea came to him. 'Perhaps Laurence was taking her out as part of his cover. Perhaps he wants to be seen to be being fair and he wants her to think she's got a chance. So he takes her out to lunch to show his even-handedness.'

Isabel considered this. It was possible, she thought, but it sounded a bit unlikely. Jamie, though, was warming to that explanation. 'I think that's what's happening,' he said. 'It's cunning. Laurence is very cunning.'

Isabel sighed. 'I'm not sure if I've been much help.'

'You have,' said Jamie. 'You've shown what a schemer he is.'

'I doubt it.' She paused. She was not proposing to do anything else about these orchestral machinations, but she was interested to know if Jamie was going to take matters further. 'So what are you going to do?'

'Me?' said Jamie. 'Nothing. You know I've always told you not to interfere in things. I'm going to follow my own advice.'

'Very few people do that,' said Isabel, and resumed her work on their dinner. The rice was now being heated in the truffle oil, while several chopped onions sizzled in butter in a neighbouring saucepan.

Very few people do that . . . And that includes me, she thought. She had decided she would go tomorrow and speak to Paul. She was not going to try to build up a picture of what was happening between him and Richard, and, by extension, with the rest of the Douglas family. She was simply going to go and speak to Paul and challenge him over the divisions he was causing in that unhappy family. Sometimes it was best to be blunt with people. Sometimes that worked, when people realised the impact of their attitudes and actions. Sometimes.

'I still feel bad about the whole thing,' said Isabel. 'I'm sorry I tried to . . . ' What was the expression? Offload?

But Jamie was sorry too. 'I'd like to apologise,' he said. 'And I mean it.'

He felt guilty. It was not for him to tell Isabel how to lead her life. If she chose to help other people, then was it right that he should interfere in the way in which she went about it? No, it was not. And now he regretted it. And yet, they were in a marriage. In a marriage, you *did* have a stake in what your spouse did – that was the whole point of marriage: it made you one, as actors within the world, and as recipients of what the world did. And with that union of agency, surely there came some entitlement at least to persuade the other person to aspire to x and to avoid y.

Except that Isabel was different. She was not just anyone. She was Isabel Dalhousie, philosopher, who spent half her waking hours thinking about how we are to live our lives; and I, who am I? Just a bassoonist who spends half *my* time going *tiddly-om-pom-pom* inside my head and the other half trying to teach youngsters how to press the right keys and observe the time of the music and pay attention to the dynamics as clearly marked on the score, which most of them ignore, and . . .

Isabel was looking at him. Now she said, 'What about you?'

And he said, 'What about me? What?'

'What about you – you're always saying to me that I don't pay any attention to what you're saying, that I daydream all the time, and what about you?'

A smile spread across Jamie's face. 'I was thinking: you're the serious one. You're the one who faces up to the difficult issues, while I just go *tiddly-om-pom-pom.*'

She stared at him in puzzlement. 'Who goes *tiddly-om-pom-pom*? Who said anything about that?'

'I do. I walk around thinking about music. That's the *tiddly-om-pom-pom* bit.'

'But you don't. Your head is full of . . . full of beautiful music. Vivaldi. Mozart.'

'Mozart? He goes *tiddly-om-pom-pom* quite a lot.' Jamie thought for a moment, and then continued, 'Of course, some composers don't. Britten doesn't. Arvo Pärt doesn't. Lots don't.

'But Mozart's wonderful anyway. And he only goes *tiddly-om-pom-pom* some of the time, and he does it rather well, if you think about it. Then suddenly he sits down and writes "Soave sia il vento" and your heart stops because it's so beautiful.'

He looked at her. He knew what she meant. They were agreed on that. That, he thought, was what was really important in a marriage: understanding what was right, whether in music or in anything else. He could never be married – not

188

truly married – to somebody who didn't agree with him on that. It would be like being married to somebody with no soul – or with the wrong sort of soul, perhaps.

A noise came from the risotto pan – the sizzling of rice in oil. Isabel attended to it. It was time to pour in the stock in which she would cook the rice.

'Risotto doesn't make itself,' she said.

But in spite of that, she left the risotto. It was only rice, after all. She left it and walked round the table to kiss him on the cheek. It was a chaste kiss – one of respect, perhaps, rather than of anything else – but it said everything that she wanted to say, and it said it rather better than words might.

He was slightly surprised. He smiled at her, and his smile said what her kiss had said. That was another way in which he was fortunate, he thought – to have somebody to smile at, to have somebody to kiss.

14

The following morning, Isabel and Jamie walked the boys to school together. Jamie and Magnus went slightly ahead, with Isabel following a few yards behind, holding Charlie's hand. He seemed to be in a good mood, chattering away about a model he was making with his construction set. It was a spaceship, he explained, and it had fourteen windows and five wheels. It was capable of travelling at 60 miles an hour, he explained – sometimes even more.

'That's very fast,' said Isabel. 'Even for a spaceship.'

'Some spaceships can do 100 miles an hour,' said Charlie. 'The Americans have got one of those.'

'They're very lucky,' said Isabel.

Charlie agreed. 'Rory says that Russian spaceships only go at 20 miles an hour.'

Isabel smiled. 'Rory must have read about that some-where,' she said. Rory, she thought ... the alleged victim. The silenced complainant. 'Tell me, did you really bite

Rory? Mummy's not cross with you, but it's best to tell the truth. Then you can say sorry. We should say sorry to the people we bite.'

For a few moments, Charlie did not respond. Then he said, 'Just a small bite. Just once.'

Isabel looked down at him. He was smiling back up at her. Butter, she thought, wouldn't melt; but it wouldn't melt in any mouth of that age, even the mouths of the guilty.

'Will you say sorry to him?' she said.

Charlie nodded.

'Promise?'

'Yes. I promise.'

'And you won't bite anybody else? Also promise that?'

'Yes. Promise. Promise. Promise.'

She continued their walk. But then, a few moments later, he said, 'Grace bit me on the nose. She should say sorry too.'

Isabel stopped in her tracks. 'Charlie, you mustn't make things up. Grace would never bite you.'

His expression was one of real outrage. 'She did. She did. She bit me on the nose – on the way back from school. I was walking along and she bit me on the nose. Magnus saw her. Ask him.'

Isabel tried another tack. 'Why would Grace bite you on the nose, Charlie?'

He answered immediately. 'Because I bit Magnus. It was his fault.'

'You bit Magnus?'

'Yes. I gave him a bite – just a little one. And then Grace said that I shouldn't bite people but she bit me herself. She bit my nose.'

Isabel looked ahead to see that Jamie and Magnus had stopped, and were waiting for them to catch up.

'We'll talk about all this later,' she said. 'But in the meantime, no biting. Do you understand? No biting – ever.'

Charlie nodded, albeit reluctantly. He wanted to get the conversation back onto a more interesting topic, which was spaceships – their trajectories, their speeds and their general possibilities.

As they entered the school grounds, Isabel went over what had just transpired. Charlie's confession was significant, and it pointed to his truthfulness. But if he were telling the truth about his having bitten both Rory and Magnus, then what conclusion could be drawn about the rest of what he had said – in other words, the accusation he had levelled against Grace? It was looking increasingly likely that there might be some truth in what he'd said about that, although it was difficult to imagine. Isabel wondered whether she should have a word with Grace. People who were accused of something had the right to know of the nature of the accusation, and also to be informed of the identity of their accuser. It would be quite wrong if I were to allow that charge to hang over Grace's head, Isabel thought, without giving her the chance to refute it.

Miss Young greeted them at the entrance to Primary One, where Jamie joined them, having dropped off Magnus at the pre-school gate. Isabel raised the issue of biting. 'I've spoken to him,' she said, her voice lowered so that Charlie would not hear.

But he did. 'I bit Rory,' he said in a loud voice, directed at the teacher. 'I'm really sorry, and I won't be bad any more.'

Isabel grinned. 'Well, that wasn't planned,' she said to Miss Young.

'I imagine not,' said Miss Young. 'Thank you. And I suggest we draw a line under this. Water under the bridge.'

But then Charlie added, 'And Grace is going to say sorry to me for biting my nose.'

Miss Young's eyes widened. She turned to Isabel for an explanation.

Flustered, Isabel said, 'I'm not sure if that happened.'

'It did,' protested Charlie.

'A misunderstanding,' said Jamie quickly.

Miss Young glanced at Jamie, 'A misunderstanding – in what sense?'

'We don't know the full circumstances,' Jamie admitted, looking at Isabel imploringly. He needed support.

'I'm going to speak to Grace,' Isabel said. 'It'll all be cleared up.'

Miss Young nodded cursorily. She did not appear convinced.

Afterwards, as they walked back to the house, Jamie said, 'Well, that was embarrassing.'

'It was,' agreed Isabel. 'But then, teachers hear all sorts of fanciful things from kids. They're used to it. They know to discount most of it.'

She remembered what a teacher friend had said about the dangers of asking young children to write stories about their home lives. That friend, who taught a class of eight-year-olds, had invited her pupils to do just that and had received this classic little essay: 'My daddy goes to the office every morning. When he comes back, Mummy shouts at him and he goes upstairs and drinks whisky.' Her friend had then said: 'It transpired that the father had dictated the essay to the child. He has a sense of humour, you see.'

Isabel and Jamie walked on.

'I'm going to go and have a word with this Paul later this morning,' Isabel said, as they reached the front door. 'You can put things off and put things off, until eventually . . .'

'. . . eventually you can put them off a little bit longer?' suggested Jamie.

'No,' said Isabel. 'That's not what I intended to say.'

'Why him?' asked Jamie. 'Why not speak to Richard? He's the source of the problem. He's the one who's going to have to come round.'

'Yes,' she said. 'If any log jams are going to be moved, he'll have to do it. But I've been thinking: neither parent has so much as addressed a word to Paul. They seem to have cut him dead. People really have to speak to one another, you know.'

Jamie agreed. 'Yes, they do. But are you sure that *you* want to?'

'I don't want to, but I shall.'

Jamie remembered something. 'I remember you once told me all about the philosophical complexities involved in the whole business of wanting to do something. You said if you didn't want to do something, but did it anyway, strictly speaking you wanted to do it – because that's what you ended up doing.'

Isabel did not remember that conversation, but she knew what she would have said. It was all to do with levels of wants: strong and weak. Strong wants involved *will* and *desire*. Weak wants involved just *will*. This was a case, she thought, of a weak want, but she did not have the time to explain that to Jamie again, as for the next three hours she would have to read through the proofs of the next issue of the *Review* before they went back to the printer in Stirling. The day could come, she suspected, when printers ceased to exist, but for the time being they were still there and she was grateful for that fact. She would miss the smell of ink, she thought, even though, for the most part, it was metaphorical. We appreciated things we did not necessarily see or touch because knowledge of their existence reassured us in some way, and because the world was better for their presence. She had never been to Machu Picchu, and she accepted that realistically she never would, but she was glad that the citadel was there. She would miss it if it were not, just as she would miss the cave paintings at Lascaux if they were to disappear, or the Ceremony of the Keys at the Tower of London, or the Book of Kells in Dublin, even if she was unlikely ever to see any of these things. Then she thought of endangered animals and rare and threatened languages. The world was a complex and lovely place, but its complexity and loveliness was everywhere under threat. We were the problem. It was as simple as that.

They heard a noise behind them. Something had moved under one of the rhododendrons. Jamie pointed silently. 'Him,' he whispered.

Isabel looked, but saw nothing. Brother Fox must be lurking somewhere, contemplating his vulpine agenda. He was another thing that she was glad existed. There was some chicken in the fridge, and she would leave it out for him.

But Jamie had already thought of that. 'You go and do your work,' he told her. 'I'll leave him some chicken.'

She reached out to touch him. He was wonderful, this man who had come into her life and transformed it. He was kind. He was everything she had dreamed of, but he was real. Jamie actually existed – living proof of the perfect. He touched her back.

'We're his parents too,' he whispered.

She shook her head. 'His siblings.'

'Not that we're sentimental. Or anthropomorphic.'

She smiled. 'Anthropomorphic? You and I? Never.' Then she added, 'I wonder if Brother Fox has a name for *us*?'

Jamie's eyes lit up, but he said nothing. How did foxes think?

Isabel was not sure. They had no language, but of course they had thoughts. And were those thoughts pictorial? Did Brother Fox think in images: of chickens, darkness, of the enemy, the oppressor – and his allies, their dogs? Did he see himself, in his sleekit splendour, a flash of russet, a moving shadow?

Isabel finished reading the proofs of the *Review* rather earlier than she had anticipated, meaning she had time to attend to at least some of the morning's mail before she left the house. The mail had been delivered by their regular postman, Graham, with whom she usually exchanged a few words as he handed her the letters and parcels that arrived for the *Review*.

'More books for review,' he said, as he handed over three large padded envelopes. 'And I hope these are subscriptions.'

Isabel examined the three letters he passed over. 'Two are,' she said. 'One's a bill, I think.'

'That's the unpleasant side of my job,' Graham apologised. 'Sorry. Bills have to get through. I like delivering birthday cards and presents. And Valentine's cards too, of course. I love delivering those.'

'Cupid,' said Isabel.

'You could say that. I do my best.'

She went inside and looked at the books. Two were concerned with environmental ethics, and one was on issues of confidentiality. There were so many books on environmental ethics now, she thought, that it must be difficult to say anything new. But then you might say the same thing about most subjects. Philosophy had been *done* – that was the problem. Everything had been *done* and scholarship was becoming more and more specialised, looking at problems in finer and finer detail. And as you did that, Isabel thought, you progressively lost sight of the bigger picture, even to the point of being able to say anything about it. There could never be another Kant, or Schopenhauer or Hume because nobody could take the broad, general view that they took – any attempt to do so today would flounder in detail, in minutiae, in the footnotes of what had gone before. Although there were still some, she thought, who were concerned with what she called general themes and who might be heard above the clamour of the particular. There were some who thought in public, as she called it, and who encouraged others to do the same. It was not always easy to take on such a role, as there were so many who did not want to listen to anything said by those with whom they might disagree, but Roger Scruton and Richard Dawkins and Tony Grayling had all done what they could to get the general public to engage with philosophical issues, and there were others. And then there was her friend, Richard Holloway, whom she saw from time to time in the fish shop; he thought of things that academic philosophy tended to ignore – questions of how we might feel about ourselves. There were still people who had not disappeared under detail.

She finished up in her study. The proofs had been electronically annotated and dispatched; letters filed; the bill – another one from the printer, and larger than last time – paid, with an inward groan. Now she was free to go.

But then Grace came in.

'You're going out?'

Isabel nodded. 'I'm going to go and see somebody at that wine shop at Holy Corner.'

Grace had been carrying a duster, which she now used to wipe the top of a filing cabinet in a desultory manner. She had not come to clean, Isabel thought.

'Oh, that place.'

'Yes. Do you know it?'

Grace shrugged. 'I don't buy anything there. Or hardly ever. But I know about one of the people there. My friend, Ellen, cleans his aunt's place.'

Isabel waited. Grace knew things that she and Jamie did not know. She had always been aware of that, and sometimes these things came out unexpectedly.

'Which person? There are two young men there, I think.'

'Yes. There's the owner – I don't know anything about him. Then there's his friend. His aunt lives in Newington.'

Isabel's interest showed.

'She has a bed-and-breakfast place there,' Grace went on. 'She's getting on a bit, though, and she's going to sell it. She's going to move to a flat in Viewforth. One of those new ones – you know, in the old school building there.'

Isabel was less interested in the aunt. 'The nephew? What about him?'

'He's called Paul.'

'That's him,' said Isabel. 'What does your friend say about him?'

Grace shrugged. 'I don't think she's said much. She sees a bit of him though, as he's often about his aunt's place. They get on very well. His girlfriend is a florist, and she gives his aunt flowers that are getting a bit too old to sell, but still look good. She passes them on. She's very considerate.'

'Whose girlfriend?' asked Isabel.

'Paul's. The young man in the wine shop. The one with fair hair. The tall one.'

Isabel said nothing as she absorbed this information. Grace knew things. She had always been aware of that.

'Do you know Paul yourself?'

'No, I don't. But Ellen likes him. She says that he's really kind to his aunt. She likes sherry, his aunt, so he gives her bottles of sherry and chocolates, and of course she gets the out-of-date flowers from the fiancée.'

Grace put down her duster. 'Actually, I wanted a word with you.'

'I'm here,' said Isabel. She knew that she would have to tackle Grace about the bite, but now was not the time.

'I'm afraid I did something I'm rather ashamed of,' said Grace, looking directly at Isabel. 'I had to speak to you about it.'

Isabel was quite still. Grace was going to confess. Thank heavens! Now there would be no need for her to raise the issue, which she had not been looking forward to doing. Suddenly there was a lot to think about: Grace's revelation about Paul having a girlfriend was certainly significant – and now a confession.

'Charlie was very difficult on the way back from school the other day,' Grace began.

Isabel inclined her head. 'Don't we all know that. He can be a handful sometimes.'

'He bit Magnus, and when I told him off, he said something very rude to me. Very rude. I'm sorry, but I snapped. I lost my temper with him and asked him how he'd feel if somebody bit *him*. Then I gave him a little nip – just to show him. I'm really sorry – I shouldn't have done it. You know how I'd normally never do anything like that.'

'Oh, Grace,' Isabel said. 'I understand. Of course, I fully understand. And it probably taught him a lesson. There are plenty of occasions when I myself have been only too tempted to bite his nose.' She felt immense relief that Grace had spoken about this; a boil had been lanced.

Grace stared at her. 'Bite his nose?'

'Yes,' said Isabel. 'He told me. He said that you bit his nose.'

Grace struggled to speak, such was her indignation. 'He said I bit his *nose*?'

Isabel nodded. 'Yes. I was a bit surprised. But then—'

'I did *not* bite his nose,' Grace said, her voice rising in anger. 'Why on earth would I bite his *nose*?'

Isabel shrugged. 'I thought you might have bent down and bitten the first bit of him you came across ...'

'I would never,' Grace protested, '*never* bite anybody's nose.' She shuddered. 'The germs. Think of all the germs that noses have. You'd get those.'

Isabel could only think of agreeing. 'You're right. It would be very insanitary.'

'He's making it up,' said Grace. 'I went nowhere near his nose. All I did was give his hand a small nip – just to show him what it felt like. That's all.'

Isabel was quick to agree. She would have to speak to Charlie again, this time about the difference between the truth and lies, which was something that very young children – and some adults (she thought of one or two in public life) – seemed to find difficult to grasp. 'Of course he's making it up. Little imp.'

'But I'm still very sorry for what I did. Even if I didn't bite his nose – which I *didn't* – I still shouldn't have given his hand that nip.'

Isabel reached out and took Grace's hand. For a moment she thought: what if I decided to bite it? But she came to her senses – and it wasn't a *real* temptation, she decided. Sometimes there was something within us, some inner voice, that goaded us with the thought that we might do something awful. We never listened, of course, but the voice occasionally still tried it on. 'Don't think about it any longer,' she said to Grace, patting her hand in reassurance. 'It's a storm in a teacup. I'm going to get Charlie to apologise and we'll forget about the whole thing.'

'I feel very ashamed of myself,' Grace persisted.

'You needn't. Nobody need feel ashamed of being human.'

Grace looked at Isabel with gratitude. 'You're very kind,' she said.

Isabel gave Grace's hand a press before releasing it. She had always been embarrassed by compliments. 'All over,' she said.

She stood outside Holy Corner Wines for a few minutes before going in. It was a large shop – twice the size of most in the immediate vicinity – with a display occupying six well-decorated windows. One of these featured a map of the Bordeaux region, with individual bottles linked, by paper streamer, to a pinpoint on the map. Another had an enlarged photograph of what Isabel recognised as the Montalcino sky-line, with, underneath it in the window, a wooden wine case from which several bottles of Brunello were protruding. A third featured whiskies, with an old sepia photograph of dis-tilleries on Islay alongside a blown-up quotation from a whisky writer referring to the flavour of peat and the reek of seaweed. Isabel had no liking for whisky, but she knew that Jamie liked the Islay malts, with their smoky flavour. A single bottle lasted him almost a year, as he only rarely poured himself a dram.

She took a deep breath and entered the shop. She was not sure how she was going to play this; all she knew was that she had a legitimate reason for going into the shop – she needed to buy a couple of bottles, but beyond that she would have to wait and see. She was hoping she would find Paul on his own; if he was not, and Richard was there, then she would have to buy a bottle of wine and return some other time.

Isabel saw immediately that there were two people on duty

in the shop, and several customers. The two staff members were a young man and a young woman – the young woman was behind the desk, at the cash register, completing a transaction, while the young man was reaching for a bottle from a shelf in order to give it to a woman standing beside him. Isabel saw that he was tall and had fair hair, which was how Grace had described him. So this was Paul.

She moved to a shelf marked 'Australia' and began to examine the bottles. Although Isabel tended to drink New Zealand Sauvignons, she liked Australian wine, particularly the whites of Margaret River. She saw that there were several of these on the shelf before her, and that under some of them a small, handwritten card had been stuck. She leaned forward to read one of them. *This comes from the banks of the Willyabrup Creek. It's only a small estate, but they know what they're doing and how! Lots of citrus. A bit of peach. One of our favourites.* And then a signature: *Paul.*

She looked at the card beneath another bottle. The label showed a koala. *Never buy a wine with a koala on the label*, an Australian friend had once said to her – and then laughed. It was not serious advice, she thought. *Grapefruit. Caramelised apple. Chardonnay pretending to be white Rioja? What's not to like? Richard.*

The koala on the label was holding on to a branch with one paw. Isabel looked more closely. In the other paw was a wine glass. She stood back. Koalas holding glasses were a little bit much – just a bit, but Australians could do irony so well when they set their minds to it.

She became aware of somebody behind her, and turned to face the young man who had been helping a customer. He was smiling at her. She noticed his teeth – perfectly straight – and his small ears, tucked under a thatch of blond hair. Small ears were said to be a sign of something, she seemed to remember, but of what exactly? There was so much folklore to forget.

She took in his clothes, which were unremarkable. He was wearing blue, working dungarees – the garb of a warehouse. A helpful name badge read *Paul*.

'We have fun with those labels,' he said. 'But remember: they're personal opinions – that's all.'

'All opinions are implicitly personal,' said Isabel.

He seemed amused. 'Of course.' And then, 'Margaret River is a fantastic region. It only started a few decades ago, but it's really important now. There are a lot of people who regard it as the best Australian region by far.'

'I like whites,' said Isabel. 'New Zealand mostly, but perhaps I should be more adventurous.'

'We have plenty of New Zealand whites,' said Paul. 'Would you like to see some?'

Isabel hesitated. 'Yes, I would. But ...'

He waited.

'But I wondered if I could have a word with you.'

Paul looked puzzled. 'About New Zealand wines?'

She shook her head. 'A private matter. Do you have an office back there?'

'Sure.' He gestured towards a door that led off beyond the whisky section. 'It's pretty small, but we've got two chairs.'

'That would be fine.'

He signalled to the young woman, who nodded before going off to attend to another customer who was waiting by a large bin display of Italian reds.

Inside the office, Paul pointed to a rickety-looking dining-room chair. 'Please sit down,' he said. 'It's not exactly comfortable.'

He took up his place behind the desk.

203

'You don't know me,' Isabel began. 'I live round the corner.'

He smiled encouragingly. 'Yes?'

'My name is Isabel Dalhousie.'

'I'm Paul.' He did not give a second name, but then, Isabel reflected, few did these days.

'I know Laura and Bruce Douglas.'

Paul stiffened. His warm manner was now replaced by reserve. 'Oh yes.'

'The parents of your colleague, Richard.'

He lowered his eyes. 'Yes, I know.'

'I don't believe you know them – I mean, not personally.'

Paul stared at her. 'You could say that.' He paused. 'But you could also say: they don't know me.'

Isabel tried to assess the effect of her words, but found it hard to judge. 'They're very distressed by the breakdown of their relationship with Richard.'

Paul sat back in his seat. 'Are you suggesting that's my fault?'

She was taken aback by the tone of his response. His manner was now quite different from before – this was no longer a friendly encounter. She sought to reassure him: 'Of course not. I'm sorry if it sounded like that.'

She saw him relax slightly.

Now he said, 'Richard has a terrible relationship with his father. He won't speak to him.'

'I gathered that,' said Isabel.

'He hates his father, I think.'

'It rather seems that way.'

Paul was fiddling with a paper clip. He had straightened it, and now he was bending it back into shape. 'I wouldn't want it to be like that. You hate people and then you find you're at their funeral and you hate yourself for hating them. I've tried to get him to patch it up, but he refuses.' He gave Isabel a searching look. 'Have you any idea why the two of them are . . . ' He shrugged. 'Are at daggers drawn?'

Isabel bit her lip. She had reached a decision. There was no point in being anything but direct. If he would be offended, then he would be offended.

'I think that Richard's father might not approve of the relationship between you and his son.'

She had said it. Now for the effect.

It was one of bemusement. 'Our relationship? What relationship? We share a flat. We work together. All that?'

'I think he believes it's more than that.'

Paul looked at her with incredulity. 'Us? He thinks that we're an item?'

Isabel nodded.

Paul burst out laughing. 'But we aren't. We just aren't. We're friends — we've been friends since university. But we're not together in that way. Richard's seeing a nurse who works in the Western General.' He shook his head in disbelief. 'Not that it matters, anyway — although it might to Richard's father, I suppose.'

'I get the impression that he thinks you and Richard are together,' said Isabel. 'And I think he feels that you've turned Richard against him.'

'Nonsense,' snapped Paul. 'Quite the opposite, in fact.' He twisted the paper clip again and the metal snapped. 'You know what I think?'

Isabel waited.

'I think that Richard wants his old man to think that. In fact, come to think of it, that makes sense. Before they parted company, so to speak, he wound him up terribly. He taunted him politically — his dad's a unionist through and through, and Richard's a Scottish nationalist.'

'And you?' asked Isabel. 'Are you with him on that?'

Paul shrugged. 'I'm not all that political. I can see the arguments – can't you? Scotland's an ancient nation. We lost our independence in 1707 and there are plenty of people who think we'd be better off getting it back. But at the same time I can also see that there are loads of people who see themselves as British and who are happy enough with that identity.'

'So you haven't tried to persuade him either way?'

'No, not at all. But I do know that he lost his cool with his dad over that. I think he probably wants to punish him for something or other.' He smiled. 'What did Freud say about the relationship between boys and their fathers?'

'He said quite a lot.'

'Yes. And I think that Richard might have taken a certain pleasure in letting his dad think we're a couple.' He seemed to warm to the theme. 'Yes, I can imagine him doing that. He knows how to get up his father's left nostril.'

Isabel sighed. 'Do you think it's reparable? Could anything be done to bring them back together?' And then, before he could answer, she added, 'Is there any particular reason why he should want to punish his father? Apart from the usual Oedipal stuff?'

It proved to be exactly the right question. Paul thought for a short time, then said, 'They had a major row a year or so ago. That was the start of it, I think.'

'About Richard's going into the family firm?'

'No. Nothing to do with that. But it was to do with the family business. A friend of Richard's applied for a job there and didn't get it. Richard was furious. He went to see his father and they had a big shouting match.'

Isabel asked him to explain.

'This friend was a really old one,' Paul said. 'He was called

Robert something or other – I can't remember his full name. But he and Richard were at school together – right from the beginning. Heriot's. They kept in touch even though Robert went down to Oxford. He was at New College, I think.'

'And then?'

'And then Robert came back to Edinburgh and started looking for a job. He'd worked on an estate in Bordeaux during the summer when he was at university. And he had an internship with Berry Brothers down in London. He wanted to be in the wine trade.'

'I can see where this is going,' said Isabel.

'Yes. He applied to Richard's family firm. Richard spoke to his father about Robert and his father, apparently, said that he saw no reason not to take him. He had all the right credentials, after all. But he said that he would need to give him an interview.'

'Which happened?'

'Yes, it did. And then, after that, Richard's father suddenly said that Robert couldn't have the job. Richard went ballistic. I've never seen him so angry. He put it all down to one thing: Robert's gay. He's quite open about it, and he told Richard that he'd mentioned it to his father at the interview.'

Suddenly it all made sense to Isabel. 'And that sunk him?'

'Yes. Richard was sure of it. He said his father was prejudiced, that this could be the only reason.'

'Very unfair,' said Isabel. 'And surprising – these days. Most people are beyond all that.'

'Yes,' said Paul, 'they are. But not him, apparently.'

'So you think that this led to the breakdown of relations?'

Paul nodded. 'It seems likely.'

Isabel thought about this. Then she said, 'So, in your view, Richard may have more or less implied to his father that you and he were in a relationship in order to confront him with the issue? To get to him?'

'Very possibly,' agreed Paul. 'And also there's the political thing. Richard is in rebellion, you know. And looking around us, who can blame him?'

Isabel said nothing. Paul was right. There was so much wrong with what we had; with our old institutions and their comfortable patterns of privilege and exploitation, with our pursuit of the material at the cost of the very planet on which we lived ... It was understandable that people might be in rebellion against all that. And here, in Scotland, there was a desire for something new, for something that the existing state seemed unable to give – a desire for a rather different future. And yet, thought Isabel, that was what every creed claimed to offer, and so many of them then ended up the same, if not worse, as those that had gone before. If she had to define herself, it would be as a gradualist; she was not a conservative – but she believed in changing things in a way that did not create new monsters, that did not take away from people their sense of who they were and where they came from. And she believed, most strongly, in fellowship and sharing, and in not denying the humanity of those with whom she might disagree. That cut out a lot from a menu that seemed to want to demonise the 'other'.

'I think he wanted to show his father,' Paul continued, 'that he was having nothing to do with his whole conservative, don't-rock-the-boat world. He wanted to put a bomb under it.'

'And he did.'

'Yes, and he did.'

Isabel rose to her feet. 'This has been very helpful.'

'Helpful to what?' asked Paul.

'It's helped me to understand what happened – or may have

happened. It might also help me to do something about it.'

'To repair the rift? Is that what you think you can do?'

'Yes.'

Paul looked doubtful. He pushed his chair back and stood up. 'It's going to have to come from his father, you know.'

Isabel said that she had already reached that conclusion. 'I agree with you. I think he's the one who has the apologising to do.'

'And will he?'

Isabel replied that she could not tell. 'Apologies can be powerful, but they don't always work. They're the first step, though.'

Paul thought about this. 'Possibly.' Then he added, 'I'm glad you spoke to me, rather than to Richard. Richard doesn't take kindly to people who interfere in his affairs. It could have been a bit . . . well, a bit dangerous.'

For a few moments, Isabel said nothing. Jamie had always warned her that one of these days she would find herself in real trouble for getting involved in the affairs of others. Had she come close to that in this case? She felt a sudden tinge of dread.

'Thanks for the warning,' she said.

Paul showed her back into the main part of the shop. 'What about that New Zealand white?' he asked.

'Please show me,' said Isabel, and added, 'Broadly speaking, I'm in favour of it.'

Paul liked that. 'Aren't we all? Or most of us, I should say.'

His mobile phone began to buzz. He took it out of his pocket and Isabel glanced at it. It displayed a photograph on its home screen. She looked away.

Paul answered, 'Richard's phone.'

A voice at the other end said something unintelligible.

'All right, I'll tell him,' said Paul, ending the call. And then, to Isabel, 'Richard leaves his phone lying about.'

'So you end up having to answer it?'

Paul smiled. 'Yes. Quite often, in fact.' He pointed to a shelf. 'Now then, Marlborough Sounds? Or something different?'

15

By the time Isabel left Holy Corner Wines it was shortly before one o'clock. For a few moments she hesitated before she made up her mind and started to walk back down Bruntsfield Place towards what she was reminding herself to refer to as Cat's old deli. She would have lunch there and catch up, if he was not too busy, with Eddie. She had heard that he was having driving lessons, which pleased her, as it was a sign of growing confidence. She had a soft spot for the young man – as did most people who had dealings with him – and although he had grown into his new responsibilities in the deli, she still saw in him a certain fragility. People like that, she thought, could go back to square one if things went wrong, and then the whole business of repairing a shattered self-image could take a long time.

After a light lunch, she would go to the Douglas house in the early afternoon. As she waited for the pedestrian crossing light to change, she made a quick call to Laura to check that she and Bruce would be in. They would be, Isabel was told.

'Does this mean you have something for us?' Laura asked.

Isabel looked up at the sky. She did not think it was what they would want. 'In a way,' she said. 'I have some information, yes.'

'Did you speak to him?' asked Laura quickly.

'Not to Richard. No.'

She felt the disappointment down the line. Most people were unaware that telephones could transmit emotion, even when nothing was said, but Isabel felt they could. People spoke of 'eloquent silence', and that was much the same thing. We did not necessarily need words to convey what needed to be conveyed.

'I'll tell you about it when I see you,' said Isabel.

The call ended, Isabel decided to put the matter out of her mind until later. Her visit, she feared, was not going to be easy, but it would mark the end of her involvement in the Douglas family's affairs – an involvement that Jamie had been quite right to counsel her against. She would be more careful in the future and would not allow herself to get drawn into the problems of others quite so easily. St Augustine's plea came to mind: *Make me chaste, Lord, but not just yet.* No, I am determined, she thought, and her resolve was of immediate effect; I am going to be much firmer after this; I shall turn people down; I shall become remote and inaccessible. And immediately she knew that she could not. You should never refuse to hear somebody in their need. You should never turn a deaf ear to pain. And if you heard them, then how could you say: I shall not help you. It was impossible. She sighed. We are all on an individual wheel of life, and that is the one on which I find myself.

It was a quieter than usual lunchtime in the deli when Isabel arrived, but Eddie was busy with a customer at the counter.

He looked up when she came in, and waved a hand in greeting. Isabel pointed to an unoccupied seat at the far end of the shop but Eddie shook his head. He pointed to another table, at which a man was sitting by himself, and signalled for Isabel to sit there. She did not recognise the man, who was looking down at a magazine spread out on the table.

Isabel was puzzled. 'There?' she mouthed.

Eddie nodded. Temporarily excusing himself from the customer to whom he was attending, he came out from behind the counter and whispered in Isabel's ear, 'That's Cat's new man. That's him. You can sit with him.'

Isabel was not ready for this. 'That's Gordon?' She sneaked a glance, and then looked away again when her eyes met his.

'Yes,' said Eddie, his voice still lowered. 'He's really nice. I've been talking to him. He and Cat are going to open a coffee shop.' He looked at Isabel; his eyes were bright. 'He said he was keen to meet you. So, here's his chance.'

Isabel was not keen to follow Eddie, but he now ushered her up to the table and introduced her to Gordon, who rose to shake hands with her.

'This is Isabel. You were wondering about her, and here she is.'

'I'm Gordon,' he said. 'Cat said that she—'

Isabel stopped him. 'I should have asked you round,' she said.

'I'm going to bring you some quiche,' said Eddie. And to Gordon, 'She likes quiche, you see.' Then, with a certain pride he added, 'I know these things.'

Isabel sat down. She glanced at Gordon. He was more or less what she had expected. Cat went for men with certain rugged good looks – she had once even been involved, for a short time, with a man who earned his living modelling underpants. Now she had done it once more, and chosen a

213

man who would not have been out of place in a catalogue for men's outdoor clothing. There was a pattern, she reflected, repeated with predictable regularity, and no doubt Gordon would fit right into it.

'Cat told you about our plans,' he said.

Isabel inclined her head. 'Yes. A shop.' She glanced over her shoulder towards Eddie. Did Eddie realise that Cat and Gordon would be competitors?

Gordon intercepted her look. 'Oh, it's all sorted out with Eddie and Hannah. Cat's spoken to them. And I was discussing it with Eddie earlier on.'

Isabel expressed her surprise. 'I thought that perhaps they might be concerned.'

Eddie shook his head. 'No. We're going to do coffee, but then coffee isn't a big part of this business, is it? We're going to do coffee and bakery items – croissants, baguettes and so on. I'm keen to do more baking, you see. I was a general chef, but I'm keen on baking, so it'll be more of a patisserie. We'll do fruit tarts – there's a big demand for those.'

He smiled as he spoke, and Isabel found herself warming to the candour and friendliness of his manner. She should not have judged him, she thought, by his looks. His manner was sympathetic – and gentle. He was different from the man who had modelled underpants, from the Irish racing driver, from Leo, with all his leonine ways.

Gordon went on to discuss the leases they had signed and the progress he had made in installing equipment. He could do all that, he said. He had worked with a kitchen installation company some years ago, and had not forgotten how to do things.

'Then you went to sea?' asked Isabel.

'Not quite. I was a volunteer in Tanzania for three years.'

This was unexpected. 'Doing?'

'Doing all sorts of things on an American mission, run by people from Missouri. There were always five or six lay volunteers, and most of them had a trade – they were carpenters or mechanics and so on. I was a general dogsbody. There was a school and a small hospital – a clinic, really. We had a sheltered workshop for albinos.'

Isabel was silent.

He shook his head, as if at an unpleasant memory. 'They can have a difficult time.'

'The albinos?'

'Yes. For a whole lot of cultural reasons, but also because of the sun. They can't go out as others can. They need special creams to protect them from the solar damage – and those are in short supply. Without them, they're at a very high risk of cancer.'

Isabel frowned. What had happened afterwards? 'But then you went off and cooked on yachts?'

'Yes. That somehow happened. You know how one's life can take unexpected turns? I found myself becoming a rather specialised sort of chef.'

'It sounds very different from Tanzania. Not the most obvious progression, if you don't mind my saying so.'

'No, it wasn't. The yachting world is very different. But now I want to settle down.' He paused and looked directly into Isabel's eyes. 'Now I've met your niece. It's odd, though, to call her "your niece". I thought you'd be much older, you see, being Cat's aunt . . . '

'You're not the first to be surprised by that,' said Isabel. 'There's not a vast gap between us.'

He sat back in his chair. 'I can't tell you how happy I am. I've been hoping for a long time to meet somebody really reliable – somebody solid and dependable. In my job, I've met rather different sorts of women, you see. On the yachts the girls were ... well, the only word is *flighty*. I know that sounds a bit old-fashioned, but they were, you know.'

Isabel swallowed. She opened her mouth to say something, but he had more to say.

'Cat and I really hit it off,' Gordon continued. 'I'd been waiting for the right person, and so had she. It worked out so well.'

Isabel swallowed again. Cat had *never* waited. Not once. Did Gordon know? Did he know about Leo and all the other men?

'I'm pretty dull,' he said with a smile. 'I'm the stay-at-home type.'

'Who's nonetheless travelled all over the world,' said Isabel.

'That's true, but ... well, I don't mind telling you, I haven't had many girlfriends. Cat's not the first, but she is the second. That's important to me.'

Isabel saw that he was blushing, and she looked down at the floor in her own embarrassment. This man knew nothing about Cat. That was clear to her. And that meant Cat must have told him nothing about her past – it was difficult to reach any other conclusion.

She looked at him. She did not think she had misjudged this man. He was as he presented himself. And now she had to deal with the issue of what you should do when somebody is about to make a terrible mistake and you, unknown to them, have information that you feel they should have.

Eddie brought Isabel her quiche. 'Cheese and mushroom, with salami and olives,' he said. 'I know you like all of those.'

Isabel thanked him. 'Eddie's having driving lessons,' she said to Gordon. And to Eddie, 'How are they going? When will you sit your test?'

Eddie sighed. 'I need more practice. But the lessons are expensive.'

Gordon looked up. 'I can take you,' he said. 'You can get some practice in my car.'

Eddie beamed with pleasure. 'Are you sure?'

'Absolutely,' said Gordon.

Eddie went off smiling, and Isabel looked at her watch. This was further evidence of the impression she had formed. Gordon was a good man.

'I'm going to have to bolt this down,' she said. 'I have an appointment.'

'No worries,' said Gordon.

'Jamie and I will have you and Cat round for dinner,' Isabel said, then added, 'Soon.'

'That would be great,' said Gordon. 'I'm looking forward to meeting Jamie.'

Isabel nodded. She felt miserable. Her life, it seemed to her, was one constant unresolved dilemma, and just as she felt she was getting to the end of one issue, another reared its head. Gordon was a good man – those years in Tanzania spoke to that. And now he was getting involved with Cat, who did not deserve somebody who had spent three years helping albinos in Tanzania. It pained her to reach that conclusion, but it was unavoidable. Cat did not deserve this man, but did that mean that she, Isabel, had a duty to warn him? No, it did not, she decided – unless, of course, he *asked*. Then it would be different. If Kant had been worried about his niece misleading some decent, meritorious Königsberg boy, then he would not have lied if the boy had asked him about her past. But that was Kant, and Königsberg; and this is me and Edinburgh, she thought. Times are different and I just don't have Kant's consistency. It cannot have been easy to be Immanuel Kant, and so I shan't try. I don't have the energy. I just don't.

But then it occurred to her that perhaps she was

217

wrong – about this and about other things. Most of us think we're right, she thought. Most of us tell ourselves that we have made sense of the world and that we understand what we see. But perhaps we don't. Perhaps we're wrong far more often than we imagine. Perhaps she was wrong about Cat. She assumed that Cat had not changed, and never would. Yet what evidence did she have for that? And even if there were to be some evidence to justify the conclusion that Cat had not undergone any road to Damascus moment and was much the same as she always was, should Isabel still deny the possibility that her niece might change in the future? Could the fact that she was now with Gordon be an indication of change on her part? Everybody deserves a chance, thought Isabel. That simple, hackneyed old saying was absolutely correct – as such simple, hackneyed old sayings so frequently are. That was why they were *old* sayings: they survived because they were true.

Before the front door at the Douglas house twenty minutes later, Isabel pressed the bell marked 'Please Pull'. A few moments later the door was opened by Laura Douglas, who greeted her with a kiss on both cheeks.

'Bruce is so looking forward to seeing you,' Laura said. 'He's been watching the clock for the last hour. He's always been the impatient type.'

'I'm not sure how much I have for you,' Isabel warned.

'But you did say you had something. You did say that, didn't you?'

'I did, yes, but let's wait until—'

'Of course. Come this way. Bruce is in the conservatory.'

Laura led Isabel through the house to a conservatory that looked out over a lawn and formal flower beds. 'There's still some summer colour left,' she said. 'We try to plan things so that we have some late-flowering plants at this time of year.'

Bruce was waiting. He sprang to his feet and advanced on Isabel. I don't want you to kiss me, she thought. He did not. He stopped short of her, and she wondered whether her body language had put him off. And her body language, she thought, might also reveal her disquiet over the conversation she felt she now had to have.

Bruce was looking at her intently. He said, 'There's something wrong, isn't there?'

Isabel held his gaze. 'Yes. There is, I'm afraid.'

'Is Richard all right?' asked Laura, her voice thin with anxiety.

'I haven't seen him,' said Isabel. 'But I assume so.'

Laura breathed a sigh of relief. 'Well, thank heavens for that.'

Bruce now invited Isabel to sit down. A tray was already on the low table in front of their wicker chairs; without asking Isabel whether she wanted tea, Laura poured her a cup.

Bruce cleared his throat. 'You can speak as directly as you like,' he said.

Isabel looked at him. 'You may not like what I have to say.'

Laura gave her husband a nervous look. 'Bruce is prepared,' she said. 'We've talked about it. We've spoken to somebody who's in a similar position.'

Isabel raised an eyebrow. She wondered what that position was. 'You mean with an alienated son?'

Laura nodded. 'That ... and the other thing. The sexuality thing.'

Bruce took over. 'Since you came to see us, we've done some soul-searching. My wife pointed out to me that I had been burying my head in the sand. I was ignoring the obvious, she said – and she admitted that she, too, was trying to put a rather different complexion on things. Not facing up to what was plainly what.'

'Yes,' said Laura. 'And we both realised that this was not the right thing to do. We're prepared to change. We're prepared to accept the situation as it is.'

Isabel took a sip of her tea. She wondered where to start.

'Perhaps I should tell you straight away,' she began. 'Richard and Paul are friends, but there's nothing more to it than that. I don't think they're lovers.'

She saw Bruce wince at the word *lovers*. But then, after his initial reaction, he gave a start, as the implications of what she had said sank in.

'I think he may have wanted you to think that he and Paul were in a relationship,' Isabel went on. 'But they don't appear to be. Paul, I'm told, has a girlfriend. As does Richard.'

'But why, then—' began Bruce.

Isabel interrupted him. 'He feels very angry with you. Yes, I'm sorry to say that, but that's what Paul said. He suggested – and I can see this as a possibility, quite frankly – that Richard feels your whole attitude is wrong. He thinks that you haven't even begun to understand where he is politically.'

Bruce made a face. 'He's all over the place. Romantic nationalism. He and his friends want a re-run of every battle we've had with the English since Bannockburn. They want to turn the clock back. The days of small states are over.'

'Bruce feels strongly about that,' said Laura.

Isabel waited a moment, and then said, 'Has it occurred to you that Richard feels equally strongly? And that he may feel you take a rather limited view of the situation.'

'He may well do,' snorted Bruce. 'But he's wrong.'

'He might say that you've closed your mind to new ideas.'

He stared at her. She waited for a riposte, but it did not come.

220

'And there's another thing,' said Isabel. 'He thinks you treated a friend of his very unjustly. He hasn't forgiven you for that.'

'What friend?' snapped Bruce.

'A school friend. One he had kept up with over the years. He applied to you for a job.'

Bruce glanced at Laura, who looked away. She knows, thought Isabel. At least she knows.

'There are business decisions to be made every day,' said Bruce. He spoke firmly, but Isabel could tell that this was bravado. Her words had struck home. He added, 'And some of these are difficult.'

Isabel faced up to him. 'I don't know anything about the circumstances of this one, but Richard feels that you discriminated against his friend on the grounds of his sexuality.'

Bruce glared at her. 'Sexuality, sexuality, sexuality – that's all we hear about these days.'

Isabel remained calm. 'Perhaps that's because we didn't listen enough in the past.'

Laura suddenly reached out for her husband's sleeve. 'Bruce, you know you were in the wrong. You told me that you—'

She was not allowed to finish. 'Not here,' he said brusquely.

But she was not to be put off. 'It was shameful. And I'm proud of Richard for standing up against it.'

Her words hung in the air, each one a dart, and each one found its target. Bruce seemed to deflate before their eyes.

Isabel looked appreciatively at Laura. 'I think your wife is right,' she said quietly. 'You did someone an injustice, and your son, to his great credit, stood up against it. Now if you are to have any hope of healing the rift that you – and yes, this is your work – have created, then you need to try to redress the wrong. You need to listen to your son – just listen to him, and even if the two of you are never going to agree, at least understand each other's views. Show each other that courtesy.'

'He needs to listen to me too,' muttered Bruce.

'He probably will,' Isabel said. 'If you say that you're sorry. I know it's hard, but it starts the process. A lot may follow from that.'

'Give Robert a job,' said Laura. 'Somebody said that he's marking time in a temporary post somewhere. Take him on – Richard will give you credit for that. Make your son proud of you.'

For a few moments, Bruce was silent. Then he said, 'I'll think about it.'

'Good,' said Isabel. 'And speaking of apologies, I'm sorry that I've been rude to you. I did exactly what I've been trying to say people shouldn't do – lapse into confrontation.'

Laura reached out to take Isabel's hand. 'Except sometimes one has to.'

'Perhaps,' said Isabel.

Isabel rose to leave. Her work was done. At the front door, Laura thanked her in a lowered voice. 'I'm so grateful to you,' she said. 'I've been feeling terrible about . . . about everything, really. About the divisions that are everywhere now – everywhere – even in families.' She paused. 'When do you think people are going to start loving one another again?'

Isabel wanted to say something helpful, but all she could say was, 'When they start.' That, she realised, was not much of an answer, but then she thought that perhaps it was.

She walked back towards Colinton Road, aware that the sky, which had threatened rain, was now clearer. The temperature of the air, she thought, was perfect. It was still the air of summer, but there was just that hint of autumn, that hint of sharpness that reminded us to appreciate what we had, to make the most of it.

She went over the events of the day – the conversation with Paul, the meeting with Gordon, and the tense and potentially confrontational discussion with Laura and Bruce. Each of these had been pregnant with risk, and yet each, in its way, had come to a resolution. The chat with Paul had been not only easy, but productive, and had revealed the troubling issue at the heart of the family rift. She remembered how, towards the end, Paul's mobile had rung – but it was not his phone, but Richard's, as he had said 'Richard's phone' and had promised to pass on a message. Then he had told her about Richard leaving his phone lying about. And she had briefly seen the home screen as he took it from his pocket and it had been a photograph of Paul, against the backdrop of the Highlands, or so she had decided. And she had not thought more about it because anyone might have a photo of himself doing something like climbing a hill – except that this was not Paul's phone but Richard's, and Richard had a photograph of Paul on his home screen. She had not thought about the implications of that.

She slowed down. What did having a photograph of some-body on your home screen actually mean? Did it suggest a relationship closer than simple friendship? She was not sure. She thought of her own phone. That had Jamie on it. When she opened it and the screen lit up, there was Jamie, pictured sitting on the lawn with a panama hat on his head, at an odd angle, and smiling. If you saw the phone, you would know immediately that its owner loved a man who sat on the grass and wore a panama hat. And Jamie's phone had a picture of her on it. She was wearing a ridiculous scarf around her neck, but he found the photograph amusing. Again, a casual observer would say: the owner of that phone loves a woman who wears silly scarves.

But was that just too simple? Human relationships had become much more fluid than they used to be. Boundaries had shifted, and people were less concerned about showing their feelings for others. Two friends who enjoyed an entirely platonic friendship might have photographs of one another on their phones. You could love a friend and yet not be in what others would call a relationship. Perhaps they were simply in a 'bromance'. David and Jonathan, she thought. And Paul had said that Richard had a girlfriend. Perhaps he did, but then what did he mean by 'seeing' someone? And could Richard have both a girlfriend *and* a boyfriend? It also occurred to Isabel that Richard might have stronger feelings for Paul than Paul had for him. Or Paul might be secretly in love with Richard, who had no idea of his feelings for him. There were so many possibilities.

She would have to think about it a bit more – but not just now. People were complex; and the human heart had room for more than one view of the world and our place in it; love had many faces, but whatever form it took, it was still love, and that was what counted. She looked up at the sky. She had done all she could. It was not for her to explore more complicated dimensions of a situation that was already well on its way to being healed.

They decided to have early dinner that night so the boys could eat with them, and to have it outside. Charlie and Magnus had a small wooden cabin at the end of the garden, half concealed by shrubs, and they asked if they could have their meal there while their parents ate on the patio.

'The beginning of their detachment,' Jamie said. 'Soon

they'll be embarrassed by us and want to walk on the opposite side of the road – you know how kids are. They don't want their friends to think that they've actually got parents.'

'Embarrassment is an inevitable stage,' said Isabel. 'We've all suffered from it. I used to be embarrassed by my father's nose. I imagined all my friends would laugh at it.'

'What was wrong with it?' asked Jamie.

'Nothing,' said Isabel. 'But when I was thirteen I thought it was the most conspicuous nose in Edinburgh.'

'But nobody bit it?' asked Jamie.

They both laughed. From the end of the garden came peals of childish laughter over some shared joke. Jamie looked at Isabel. 'Bless their innocent little hearts,' he said.

He poured them each a glass of wine. Reading the label, he said, 'Margaret River. Western Australia.' He took a sip. 'This is lovely.'

'Citrusy,' she said, smiling. 'Peach. A bit of flint.'

Jamie said, 'Something odd happened today.'

She put down her glass. 'I could say the same thing of my day. In fact, several odd things happened.' She lifted her glass. 'But you tell me first.'

'The chamber orchestra made the appointment, and they chose the player who deserved to get it: Annette – the really great musician.'

Isabel tried to recall which one that was. 'The one who wasn't having the affair with the conductor?'

'We thought she wasn't, but it transpired she was.'

Isabel asked him to explain.

'Laurence must have felt that it would look suspicious if he appointed his lover – even if she was the one who really deserved the job. So he laid a false trail. He trailed a rumour in front of the Mouse, who took it up and spread it about. So he let people believe that he was seeing Athene, but he wasn't – or not seeing her in *that* sense. And all the time he was intent on his real girlfriend getting the job.'

'Which she deserved to get anyway?'

'Precisely.'

'How ridiculous,' said Isabel.

'Precisely. But you know something? Life is ridiculous – a lot of the time.'

'Ridiculous?' said Isabel. 'Yes. Probably. But so precious.'

Was there anything wrong in what had happened in Jamie's orchestra? The right result had been achieved, after all. She thought of something. *'Murder in the Cathedral,'* she said.

'Eliot?'

'Yes. The only lines I remember from the play: *The last temptation is the greatest treason: to do the right deed for the wrong reason.'*

'I seem to remember that too,' said Jamie. 'But I'm not sure I've ever understood it.'

'There are some things we never understand,' said Isabel. 'I suspect we each have a small list of things that pass our understanding.'

Jamie looked up at the sky. He saw a trace of cloud; not much: ice crystals falling at a great height, that's what those wisps of white were. And here, below, was Scotland, our small bit of an earth that we should all share and over which we should not be fighting.

'That pass our understanding.' He echoed the words that Isabel had just used, and thought of their source – the great trove of poetic language that had been left to us by Thomas Cranmer and others from all those centuries ago. He thought of how people handed language down, generation to generation, as a gift.

'Yes,' said Isabel; simply that: 'Yes.'

There was no more beautiful form of English than the prose of that time. We had never improved on that language, she thought, and we never would. We needed poetry in our lives – poetry and love. Each was equally necessary, and there, in her garden, in those last sweet days of summer, she thought that she had both.

Alexander McCall Smith is the author of over one hundred books on a wide array of subjects, including the award-winning The No. 1 Ladies' Detective Agency series. He is also the author of the Isabel Dalhousie novels and the world's longest-running serial novel, 44 Scotland Street. His books have been translated into forty-six languages. Alexander McCall Smith is Professor Emeritus of Medical Law at the University of Edinburgh and holds honorary doctorates from thirteen universities.